Tiny Tim's
Christmas
Carol

Another Untold Miracle of Charles Dickens's Classic

Leonard Szymczak

GPS BOOKS

Praise for Leonard's First Christmas Story

"*Bob Cratchit's Christmas Carol* will inspire you to let go of the past, awaken your true purpose, and create miracles."

— Jack Canfield, *New York Times* bestselling author of *The Success Principles*™ and cocreator of the *Chicken Soup for the Soul*® series

"Leonard Szymczak presents a superbly resonant, intelligent, and charming addition to the Dickens classic, and one which celebrates the original style and atmosphere of Dickens himself but also seeks to convey more complex messages about the nature of true happiness."

— Readers' Favorite®

Praise for
Tiny Tim's
Christmas
Carol

"A sweet and beautiful addition to *A Christmas Carol* by Dickens. In this heartwarming rendition, Tiny Tim learns how to overcome hardship and embrace the Spirit of Christmas."

— Brandon Hall, co-author of *The Success Principles Workbook* with Jack Canfield, cocreator of the *Chicken Soup for the Soul*® series, and Janet Switzer

"As a lifelong Dickens's fan, especially of *A Christmas Carol*, I've been enchanted by the different iterations of this story. Leonard now brings Tiny Tim to life in a way Dickens would have loved. This is even more delightful than *Bob Cratchit's Christmas Carol*."

— Mary Harris, author of *Diggz and Wrrrussell* series

"Leonard's gift of imagination makes characters and places come alive. The Spirits of Christmas Past, Present, and Future now appear to Tiny Tim in this delightful perspective that helps him close the door to suffering and open the door to love and happiness."

— Arthur Tassinello, author of *Your Key to Love and Happiness*

"Fans of Leonard Szymczak's award-winning novella, *Bob Cratchit's Christmas Carol*, will be pleased to know that, once again, the author has used the classic by Dickens and his considerable insights as a psychotherapist to create a touching story about the true meaning of Christmas and the healing power of love."

— Anne Moose, author of *House of Fragile Dreams*

"Leonard gives us an early Christmas present with his creative spinoff of *A Christmas Carol* by Charles Dickens. This endearing story has unique, child versions of the three Spirits appearing to Tiny Tim who despairs about his broken body and wishes he could be like other children. Tim has to learn, like most of us, to change his way of thinking to receive miracles. This book will touch your heart, mind, and soul!"

— Tutti Taygerly, author of *Make Space to Lead: Break Patterns to Find Flow and Focus on What Matters*

"I love *Tiny Tim's Christmas Carol*. It's another heartwarming twist on Charles Dickens's novella. Leonard weaves his understanding of spirituality and psychology into a compelling story as angelic beings help Tiny Tim rise above his physical pain and mental suffering and embrace his true essence which is love."

— Mari Frank, author of *From Victim to Victor, Safeguard Your Identity*, and coauthor of *Fighting for Love: Turn Conflict into Intimacy*

"A must read for fans of Charles Dickens. A new twist on a famous tale that you'll be a scrooge to miss."

— Peter Gray, author of *Rough Cut, Brilliant Cut*, and *The President's Cut*

"That master weaver of stories, Leonard Szymczak, gives us another wonderful page turner in *Tiny Tim's Christmas Carol*. What's more fun than reading a heartwarming Christmas story with a message of love?"

— Danna Beal, author of *The Illuminated Workplace: Shining a Light on Workplace Culture*

"Leonard Szymczak has written another delightful and moving variation of *A Christmas Carol* that brings the lessons of Christmas Past, Present, and Future into the 21st century. Tiny Tim's story is a heartwarming update that readers, young or old, will find inspiring!"

— Rick Broniec, author of *A Passionate Life: 7 Steps for Reclaiming Your Passion, Purpose, and Joy* and the bestselling *The Seven Generations Story: An Incentive to Heal Yourself, Your Family, and the World*

"Snuggle into your comfortable recliner and read this enchanting story with some of Dickens's memorable characters. In this version, childlike Spirits visit Tiny Tim so that he, along with the readers, can discover the true meaning of Christmas."

— R. M. Morgan, author of Harriett Roth and Dan Gannon murder/mystery series

This is a work of fiction. It draws upon some of
the names, characters, and events as portrayed
in *A Christmas Carol* by Charles Dickens.

Library of Congress Control Number: 2022918296

Author: Szymczak, Leonard

Title: *Tiny Tim's Christmas Carol: Another Untold
Miracle of Charles Dickens's Classic*

Published by GPS Books, Dana Point, California, 92629

ISBN: 979-8-9869027-0-8 (paperback)
ISBN: 979-8-9869027-1-5 (e-book)
ISBN: 979-8-9869027-2-2 (hardcover)

Cover Design: Fiona Jayde
Interior Design: Tamara Cribley
Editors: Mary Harris & Glenda Rynn
Author of "Artwork" by work made
for hire: Leonard Szymczak
Author Photo: Esperanza H.S. Photography Department

Printed in the United States of America

1. Fiction/Holidays. 2. Fiction/Christian/Classic & Allegory.

Other Books by Leonard Szymczak

*Bob Cratchit's Christmas Carol: The Untold
Miracle of Charles Dickens's Classic*

Kookaburra's Last Laugh

Cuckoo Forevermore

The Roadmap Home: Your GPS to Inner Peace

Fighting for Love: Turn Conflict into Intimacy
Coauthored with Mari Frank

"Accept the things to which fate binds you, and love the people with whom fate brings you together, but do so with all your heart."

— Marcus Aurelius

Christmas Prelude

hether you know it or not, my dear reader, you are in need of a miracle! That is why you are reading this book. You may protest, thinking you merely seek a Christmas story that puts you in a festive mood. However, I can assure you, my friend, that you wish to experience a miracle.

Now I must confess that I once believed miracles belonged to the minds of children. They are more susceptible to outlandish whims and fancies, imagining Christmas as a time when presents magically appear at their doorstep or under the tree. Sadly, many suffer the pain of disappointment, the despair of loneliness, and the heartache of feeling unloved.

Fortunately, Christmas gives us a chance to open our hearts and minds to miracles. After all, three wise men received guidance to follow a star that illuminated a miraculous event, an event that changed the course of humanity. If the birth of a Child could radically alter history, then surely Christmastime could bring miracles, especially to those in need.

This story, my dear reader, is about one such person, a young boy wracked with pain. At times, the agony became so unbearable, he wished his life was over. During one of his darkest moments, he was in desperate need of a miracle.

Chapter One
Tiny Tim

In a rundown part of London in 1843, Tiny Tim, as his parents referred to him, woke up before everyone else on Christmas Eve. The six-year-old boy felt cramped in the bed that he shared with his two brothers — Matthew, older by a year, and Peter who at eleven was the eldest boy in the family. Wincing with pain, Tim slowly wriggled his way to the edge of the bed, not an easy task. Having been born with a medical condition that made his bones soft and weak, his body ached with every movement.

"Go back to sleep," whispered Peter from the other side of the bed. "It's still dark."

Despite the pain, Tim gushed, "'Tis Christmas Eve!"

"Barely," said Peter.

"Grrr." Matthew elbowed Tim in his ribs. "Quit talkin'."

"Ouch," cried Tim, an undersized boy, pale and bony. When Matthew, sandwiched between his brothers, elbowed him again, this time more fiercely, Tim yelped.

"Cut it out," hissed Peter.

While Tim avoided conflict, the hot-tempered seven-year-old Matthew did not. He resented the attention that Tim received because of his malady. As the fifth of six children, Matthew grumbled about being overlooked and took it out on his brother. That only made others feel sorrier for Tim, who rarely complained. This infuriated Matthew. A stronger and healthier boy, he mercilessly picked on his brother when his parents weren't around.

Elbowing Tim in the ribs again, Matthew growled. "Grrr. You're wakin' me."

"Stop it!" hissed Peter.

Tim slid off the crowded bed and quickly relieved himself in the chamber pot. He then started the arduous task of dressing himself in his worn and patched black trousers and oversize grey shirt. Wincing in pain, he put on the threadbare hand-me-downs from Matthew who had received them from Peter. The oversized clothes made him look even tinier.

He grimaced when he fastened the iron braces to his pant legs that were reinforced with heavy patches to prevent the metal from wearing through the fabric. While the metal frames enabled him to walk, he still needed a scruffy wooden crutch for added support. Any tumble took a savage toll on his frail bones and caused excruciating pain, so he took extra care whenever he moved.

Though his body throbbed most of the time, he rarely complained aloud. Sympathy was the last thing that Tiny Tim sought. He didn't want anyone to worry, especially his father who carried the weight of responsibility as the provider of the large family. Yet, even with that burden, Bob Cratchit treated his son with loving kindness, carrying him on his shoulders whenever they left the house.

Hobbling toward the stone-cold fireplace, Tim glanced at the window not yet illuminated by the rising sun. He shivered as he waited for his father to wake up and start a fire.

The tiny four-room house was the only home Tim had ever known. With one small room as the kitchen, another served as the hub of the house with the fireplace and dining table. Two other rooms were converted into bedrooms, one for Tim and his two brothers and the other for his three sisters and his parents, though his mother had strung a curtain to separate the girls from their parents' bed.

"Up so early," whispered his father.

Tim's eyes widened. "'Tis Christmas Eve!"

Bob Cratchit ruffled his son's unruly mop of brown hair. "Indeed! And a very fine Christmas we shall have!"

The sight of Tiny Tim waiting for him by the fireplace warmed Bob's heart. He felt a close bond with his son as a kindred spirit, for both put on a brave face when confronted with hardship.

A short man with unkempt black hair and muttonchop sideburns, Bob kissed the top of Tim's head. "Let's get some coals burning, shall we?"

His son's tiny hand reached down and grasped a lump of coal from the bin.

Bob remarked, "You've chosen a fine piece of coal, indeed."

Even though all the lumps looked the same, his father's typical comment brought a smile to Tim's face.

Completing their early morning ritual, Bob cleared the debris from last night's fire. He then placed Tim's lump of coal at the center of the fireplace and surrounded it with chunks of coal. Then he repeated the same prayer along with his son that they uttered every morning.

"May the light of God be with us today," they said in unison.

With the lighting of the fire complete, Tim asked, "Father, can you come home early today? 'Tis Christmas Eve!"

Bob thought of his employer and cringed. Ebenezer Scrooge reviled Christmas, so much so that the miser piled on extra work to make up for Bob's absence on the holiday.

"I'm afraid I'll have to work late, son."

"Maybe Mr. Scrooge will let you leave early."

Bob sighed. "I'm afraid not." Having worked for Scrooge for twenty long years for scant compensation, Bob knew him as a coldhearted man who greedily managed his wealth and possessions even down to the bucket of coal. He was lucky to burn one lump at a time as Scrooge never indulged in excess. preferring a frosty office.

"I must get ready," said Bob, his shoulders slouching. "It will be a very long day, indeed."

Tim placed a withered hand on his father's arm. "I pray for a miracle, Father, that Mr. Scrooge treats you kindly."

Bob patted his son's head. "'Tis Christmas. Never you worry."

But Tim did worry. About the pain that was getting worse and about getting bullied by his brother and the other boys in the neighborhood. But he mostly worried about his father who, like Tim, rarely complained. Even though his father maintained a brave front for a life of servitude and misery at work, Tim, the ever-sensitive soul, did not miss the slouched shoulders, furrowed brow, and exhausted look when his father returned home from work.

Following his father's example, Tim did not complain. Walking a few steps often brought intense agony, even with the support of metal braces and a crutch. While he presented an optimistic demeanor, he often felt despair. He dared not tell others about the terrifying nightmares with monsters and certainly not his daily thoughts of death.

When his father left the room, Tim warmed his small hands over the fire. Before the other children rose, he relished the quiet times in the morning. He watched the flames flicker with sparks rising in the fireplace. He imagined himself as one of those sparks, like a free spirit, ascending into the sky.

His time alone was interrupted when his mother hung the kettle over the fire to boil water for Bob's tea. With a white kerchief over her head and a fresh apron over a well-worn gray dress, Emily Cratchit prepared breakfast of porridge and tea. Because it was Christmas Eve, she added a few apple slices.

The home in Camden Town was furnished simply. The only sign of luxury was the coal in the bin that warmed the house during the frigid winter spells. Christmastime, however, was a time to splurge and that meant a wonderful meal.

"Come on, son," said his father, stirring Tim from other worldly thoughts. "Have something to eat."

He moved to the table where his father lovingly eased him onto a stool next to him. The eldest of the children, Martha, wearing a plain brown cotton dress, helped her mother serve breakfast. Working as a milliner, she would leave with her father.

"Tomorrow will be the best Christmas ever," announced Tim.

Bob smiled as did his wife.

"Indeed, son. Do you have a Christmas wish?"

Tim hesitated then replied timidly, "Why, yes."

"What is it?"

Actually, Tim wished for a different body but told his father, "That I have the best Christmas ever." In Tim's mind, that wasn't a lie. The best Christmas would give him healthy limbs.

Bob smiled. "That we shall have, son." He added, "We shall go to church late in the evening as always and pray for your health."

What his father dared not say was that without money and a doctor's care, his son might not see his next birthday. The steady decline had become evident. Bob noticed Tim's anguish whenever he walked, prompting him to carry his son whenever they went out. What concerned Bob lately was Tim's napping. He was spending more time in bed during the day.

What Tim did not say was that the naps helped him forget about his aching body. Asleep, he would sometimes enter a dreamy world where he often met angelic beings who offered him comfort. *Oh, if only I could live in that other world*, he thought.

As his father bundled up for the wintry air, his mother handed him his top hat. "Don't let Mr. Scrooge keep ye working into the wee hours."

Bob kissed his wife's forehead. "I'll come home as soon as I can." He gave her a broad smile. "But I don't know how I'll finish my work with thoughts of your Christmas pudding on my mind."

She gave him a gentle shove. "Off with ye, then."

"Come on, Martha, your mother has spoken."

His daughter grabbed her grey woolen coat and wrapped it tight around her body. She nodded to her father who opened the door. They both shivered at the morning's frigid air as they left for the day. Mrs. Cratchit watched them for a moment through the window, then returned to the kitchen where she filled the kettle for another round of tea. Belinda and Lucy joined her while Peter dragged his snoozing brother out of bed.

"I wanna sleep," grumbled Matthew.

"Fine," said Peter. "Miss breakfast."

The horror of missing out on food struck Matthew like a lightning bolt. He quickly crawled out of bed and dressed himself.

Over breakfast, Emily Cratchit passed out orders for the day. The house had to be cleaned—which wasn't that difficult for there were only four rooms. The girls would help in the kitchen and the boys would fetch a Christmas tree.

"A real tree?" asked Tiny Tim.

His mother nodded. "We don't have much to spend, but yer father wanted to make this Christmas special." She reached into a jar on a shelf and removed a coin. Handing it to Peter, she said, "See what ye can get for this."

The eleven-year-old boy gazed at the farthing in his hand. He would be lucky to get two branches for that. "I'll do my best, Mother," he said with some trepidation.

"Can I go?" asked Tim.

"Ye have to conserve yer energy," she answered.

"Yeah," scowled Matthew, revealing a chipped front tooth, the result of a fistfight in the neighborhood. His furrowed brow always made him look and act as if he had fallen out of the wrong side of the bed.

"Stay and help the girls," he added sarcastically. He didn't want a disabled brother slowing him down.

Tim flashed an angelic smile at his mother. "I don't wanna miss the fun," he pleaded. "I can rest after we get the tree. 'Tis Christmas."

She gazed at her son clutching his crutch. Reluctantly she said, "Alright. But hurry home."

"Does he have ta come?" groused Matthew, fearing he wouldn't have time to visit the toy shop.

"Yes," said his mother. "Now scoot. I have work to do." She wiped her hands on her apron and turned to Belinda and Lucy. "Girls, to the kitchen."

"Come on," beckoned Peter. He wrapped a brown scarf with the letter P stitched on it in yellow wool around his neck. After buttoning up his black coat, he announced, "We better leave before the trees are taken."

Tim grabbed his brown cap while his mother tenderly draped around his neck the brown scarf she had knit for him marked with the letter T. "Stay warm."

Rubbing his face against the woolen fabric, he gushed, "I love my scarf."

That brought a smile to Emily Cratchit for she had lovingly knitted the scarves of all her children and stitched each one with an initial in yellow wool to mark the owner.

As Tim and Matthew clutched their scarves and coats, bracing themselves for the icy wind, Peter opened the door. The fire flickered as they followed Peter out of the house.

Matthew scurried past his older brother who patiently waited while Tim hobbled as fast as his legs would allow. After walking several blocks, the three boys reached a dirt lot where a few scraggly trees littered the ground.

Eyeing the few remaining trees, none of them appealing, Peter took a deep breath and puffed up to look taller. He approached a grimy vendor warming his hands over a fire burning in a metal pot.

Speaking with as much confidence as he could muster, Peter approached him. "I want to purchase a good tree." He removed the farthing from his pocket and showed the seller.

The man blew into his dirty hands and eyed him warily. "Git. Not givin' away trees."

"Tomorrow's Christmas," said Peter. "Most have bought their trees." He pointed to a small gangly fir. How about that one?"

"Git," he said. "Waitin' for last minute shoppers."

"Ratbag," cursed Matthew. He kicked one of the trees.

Enraged, the man yelled, "Git!" He picked up a stick and was ready to strike Matthew when Tim hobbled forward.

"Please, sir," he pleaded. "Is there nothing you could give us?" He offered an innocent smile that would melt an icicle. "'Tis Christmas."

The scruffy man peered down at the braces attached to the tiny boy's legs, then at the crutch, then back at Tim's beguiling smile.

"Please, sir?" asked Tim.

The man's heart melted for a brief instant. "Awright," he grunted. He pointed the stick at a small, spindly tree naked but for a few branches and falling pine needles and muttered, "Ye ken 'ave that one."

The three boys glanced at each other in horror.

"Is that the best you can do?" asked Peter.

Before the man retracted his offer, Tim quickly agreed. "Thank you, sir. And would you mind if we had some of those broken branches?" He aimed a tiny finger at a pile of branches.

"Usin' 'em for wreaths," grumbled the man.

Before Matthew said something to quash the deal, Tim asked, "We need only two."

"Awright. Take 'em and git."

Peter reluctantly gave the man the farthing and picked up two branches.

The man glared at him. "Eh, not them." He pointed at a pile of pine castaways and scowled. "Those."

Upset at getting the leftovers, Peter snatched two branches which were more like large twigs then picked up the spindly tree as if it had a disease. He hissed a sarcastic "Merry Christmas."

Leaving the lot, Tim tried to cheer up his brother. "The extra branches and the paper ornaments will hide the empty spaces."

Peter grimaced. "It won't look good."

"But we have a tree. Better than last year!"

"Hmm," nodded Peter begrudgingly. He handed Matthew the branches. "Hold these."

His brother reluctantly took hold of the branches and sneered at Tim who, because of his infirmity, never carried anything. And when his father was with him, he became the beneficiary of his father's shoulders. To Matthew, that seemed grossly unfair. He wanted to ride tall on shoulders too, but that was reserved for his crippled brother. Resentful at the loss of privileges and the extra burden he had to carry, though branches weren't really a burden, he swished Tim with one of the branches.

Tim winced but tried to smile. "Do you want me to carry a branch."

His genuine willingness to carry one with his free arm irked Matthew. He hated how his brother charmed others, just as he did with the tree vendor.

His friendly, genial manner coupled with his frail body meant Tim received lots of attention. The only way Matthew got noticed was through fighting, mostly with his ever-so-nice brother.

He swished Tim's leg again.

"Cut it out," complained Peter. "I see what you're doing."

Matthew smiled coyly, exposing his chipped front tooth. "What? I did nothin'."

Before Peter could argue, he stopped in his tracks. Heading toward him was Billy Pecksniff and his three cronies. At twelve, Billy was one year older than Peter. With his father as a lawyer, he lived a pampered life.

Approaching the Cratchits, Billy taunted them. "The Crutchits are coming! What do ya 'ave here?"

He reached for the scraggly tree, but Peter put it behind him as if it were now a prized possession. "Leave us be."

He wanted to call the Pecksniff boy "Sniffy" just as others did behind Billy's back but after surveying his three brawny companions, Peter knew that would end badly for him and his brothers.

Billy eyed the scraggly tree. "I see ya 'ave another crutch."

"Haw, haw," snorted the other boys.

Hoping to avoid a fight, Tim began hobbling past them.

Billy tripped him with his foot, and Tim crashed to the ground.

"Haw, haw," laughed Billy and his cronies.

"What's going on," bellowed a man wearing a black coat and shiny top hat.

The boys turned and spotted Scrooge's nephew rushing toward them. "I saw you trip little Tim," scolded Fred.

"I did no such thing," lied Billy. "He must've tripped on his own because of his gimpy legs."

Fred glared at the liar. "Be off with you. I know your father. He'll soon hear of this."

Billy and the three other boys grumbled as they left, but not before Billy whispered to Tim, "See ya later, Crutchit."

Fred helped Tim up. "Are you okay?" he asked.

"I'm fine, sir," he said, but his shaking body, scraped hand, and torn trousers from landing on the ground belied his statement.

Fred steadied the little boy on his feet. "Do you need help getting home?"

Tim displayed his beguiling smile. "No, sir." He tapped his crutch on the ground. "This'll get me home."

Fred patted the lad's shoulder. "I'm on my way to visit my uncle. I'll wish your father a Merry Christmas when I see him." He glanced down the street to be sure Billy and his companions had turned a corner. "Better be off lest they return."

He tipped his top hat before departing. "Merry Christmas."

"Let's go," beckoned Peter.

"To the toy shop," shouted Matthew.

While he normally would have returned home promptly just as his mother told him, Peter felt dreadful about the skirmish with Billy and about failing to bring home a good tree. A visit to the toy shop and the Christmas display would uplift them.

He faced Tiny Tim. "How are you?"

His brother winced but nodded. "Fine. To the shop."

"We'll only have a quick look," said Peter.

The boys hurried as fast as Tim's little legs allowed them, but the image of toys brought a surge of energy to Tim. When they reached the shop, the three of them huddled in front of the glass window next to several children gazing at an assortment of toys guaranteed to delight a child's fancy. A decorated Christmas tree sparkled with shiny glass orbs.

Matthew spotted a toy drum and tapped on the window. "I want that!"

Peter eyed an elaborate chess set with the pieces carved out in wood while Tim squinted at a box with the unusual word "Thaumatrope" engraved on it. Tiny discs rested against the box.

"Aye, kin ye spare me one of yer scarfs?"

Startled, the three boys turned around and faced a beggar. Wearing dirty rags for clothes, the man wrapped his arms around his body for warmth. Ogling Peter's scarf, he poked a finger out of a pile of filthy bandages and pointed. "Kin ye spare that one?"

Peter clutched the woolen scarf. "We better be off," he told his brothers. He nudged them away from the shabby beggar as if he had a contagious disease. "Mother will be worried."

Matthew quickly followed his brother, stepping away from the man. Tim, however, kept staring at him, mesmerized. He saw pain and suffering, something he, himself, faced every day. Without another thought, Tim removed his own scarf and handed it to the beggar.

The man felt the soft wool against his cheek. "Yer a good lad."

With the prized piece of clothing marked with the letter T wrapped around his neck, the beggar shambled down the street. When Peter and Matthew rushed back to fetch Tim, they were horrified at the sight of the beggar clutching the scarf.

"Ya idiot," bellowed Matthew. "He'll sell it for whiskey."

Tim shook his head. "'Tis Christmas."

"Harumph!" carped Matthew.

"Let's go," said Peter. "Mother will be worried." Though he didn't say it, he knew she'd be angry about Tim's fall and the missing scarf.

"I wanna see the toys!" yelled Matthew.

Tim was about to say something Christmassy, but his energy gave way. He faltered in the cold.

Peter caught him before he fell. With one arm holding Tim and the other clutching the tree, Peter motioned for them to move. Treading more slowly now, the trio trudged home without further incident. When they arrived, their mother rushed to greet them.

"Where have ye been?" she asked. "I've been worried sick." When she saw Tim's torn trousers, she gasped. "What happened?"

"I'm okay," said the little boy in a weary voice. "Just a scratch."

"We came upon Sniffy and his pals," declared Peter. "He tripped Tim."

When his mother heard the details of the altercation, she fumed, "If it weren't for Christmas, I would go right over to the Pecksniffs and give them a piece of my mind."

"And Sniffy called us Crutchits," seethed Matthew. He hated the name and blamed Tim and his gimpy legs for the bullying he also received from Pecksniff.

"But Mr. Scrooge's uncle helped us, Mother," said Tim, trying to calm everyone. "And we have a tree!"

For the first time, she noticed the tree.

Embarrassed, Peter lifted the scraggly pine tree.

"Paper ornaments, a string of berries, and the extra two branches will make it look better," offered Tim before anyone complained."

"Tim gave away his scarf," Matthew announced, seizing the opportunity to tattle on his brother. "The special one ya knitted."

"What?" exclaimed his mother.

Tim raised his eyes toward her. "If it wasn't for Christmas, the poor wouldn't be clothed."

"Yes, but—"

"He gave it ta a beggar," interrupted Matthew, his eyes pleading for his mother to berate his brother. "He'll sell it for whiskey."

She pursed her lips and stopped herself from admonishing Tim for giving away his clothes. That conversation would come after Christmas.

"Aren't ya goin' to punish him?" demanded Matthew, his face turning red with anger.

"That'll be enough," she told him. She faced Tiny Tim who was leaning on his crutch and breathing heavily. "Let's clean ye up," she said. "Ye must rest and save yer energy for the festivities."

Similar to her husband, Emily fretted over Tim's condition and hoped he would make it to his seventh birthday. She brought him to the kitchen and washed his scraped hand and checked his knee where his trousers had ripped. Only a minor scratch. She gave him hot tea to warm his body. After he finished the drink, she helped him hobble to the bedroom where she eased him out of his shoes and braces. Lifting him onto the bed, she covered him with a blanket and ruffled his shaggy hair.

"Sleep, little one," she whispered,

Exhausted, he soon fell into a deep slumber.

Chapter Two
The First Spirit

*A*t five p.m., the family gathered for a light meal, saving their appetite for the Christmas feast that usually occurred around midnight, a Cratchit tradition established because of Scrooge. Since the coldhearted miser forced Bob to work late on Christmas Eve, Mrs. Cratchit postponed the feast until after her husband arrived home and had taken Tim to church.

Wiping her apron, she checked on her son. Tim was sound asleep. Rather than waking him, she left him alone in the bedroom. Since the earlier outing had depleted his energy, she wanted her son to regain some strength.

As had so often occurred, dreams flooded Tim's mind. He rarely shared his visions with his family for fear of being mocked by Matthew who often told him he was soft in the head like his bones. Yet, for the most part, Tim relished his dream world, for it comforted him with beatific figures in tranquil scenes of forests, lakes, mountains, and oceans. The occasional nightmares with monsters eating his limbs terrified him, but mercifully, most dreams gave him a respite from pain. And he never went hungry in his dreams, not like in real life.

On this particular Christmas Eve, the young boy was about to experience miracles. As he slumbered, he found himself entering a foggy mist. The sun grew brighter and burned away the haze. In the center of a lush meadow a young girl, about the same age as Tim, waved to him.

Dressed in a red dress with ruffles and decorated with evergreen garlands, she had dark-brown skin and a bright aura surrounding her face. Little twinkling bells were woven into black hair separated into two frizzy buns, each perched on one or the other side of her head. Approaching him with a bright smile, she exuded a scent of pine as she playfully waved a branch of fresh green holly.

Tim sniffed the pine, which was most unusual for he never remembered smelling a fragrance in a dream. He asked, "Who are you?"

The little girl giggled. "The Spirit of Christmas Past. Older folk call me Angelica. But young'uns call me Angel." She waved her branch in a beckoning way. "Come," she said, offering her free hand. "Let's play in your past."

Unafraid of this apparition, Tim grabbed her hand to steady himself, for in this dream he still wore braces and leaned on a crutch.

"You don't need your stick," said the girl. She gently eased it out of his hand and tossed it to the ground. "Anything can happen in a dream."

Tim wobbled and reached out for her.

Grabbing his arm, Angel asked, "Do you want to visit heaven?"

Tim winced. "Am I about to die?"

"No, silly. You don't have to die to be in heaven. Look around." She waved the branch at the lush meadow with bright yellow sunflowers and at the herd of deer munching on grass. They casually raised their heads and smiled.

"The dream world feels as if I'm in heaven," he told Angel. "Except when there's monsters."

She poked him in the ribs with her branch of holly. "You don't care for monsters?"

Tim shook his head vigorously. "Would you? They're scary."

She laughed. "Why did you create them?"

Confused by her question, he asked, "Did I make them? And did I make you?"

Angel tapped Tim on the head with the branch. "You brought me, and monsters for that matter, to wake you up."

He shook his confused head. "I don't want monsters. They scare me."

She giggled again. "Getting scared can be fun!" She waved the holly as if it was a magic wand. "Let's visit the past."

The meadow and deer faded, and in their place a light radiated from nowhere and everywhere. A warm glow pulsated through Tim. His braces fell away, as did his legs. What shocked him the most was that his entire body disappeared!

"Wh-where am I?" he asked alarmed.

"The past," answered Angel.

"Wh-what happened to my body?"

The young girl laughed. "You believe you're a body. That's not true. Well, only a little. But that's not who you are or where you come from."

Tim checked for his hands and feet but saw nothing. "Where's my body?"

"You don't need one here. When your soul came to Earth, you dressed yourself with clothes of flesh and bones."

"Soft bones," he added, "and a crippled body." He stared at the apparition. "And how come I see you but not me?"

Angel chuckled, causing the bells in her frizzy hair to jingle. "There are no physical shapes in heaven."

Tim stared at the otherworldly figure with a bright aura surrounding her dark-brown face. Her ruffled red dress sparkled with evergreen garlands.

"If there are no shapes in heaven, why do I see jingle bells in your hair?" He sniffed again. "And why do you smell like a Christmas tree?"

Angel's eyes twinkled. "It's *your* dream. I appear in a form that's familiar."

He stared at her brown face. "I don't know any girls who look like you."

She laughed. "Maybe not in *this* lifetime, but we come from the same place." She waved the branch. "Come. we have lots to see before your other visitors arrive."

"Other visitors?"

"The Spirit from Christmas Present has gifts for you, and Christmas Future will show you what may be."

"But I wanna see myself," said Tim, feeling naked without a body.

"How?"

"Like I am."

"Just as you are on Earth?"

"Why, yes."

"If you want to feel your old self, so be it." She tapped him with the branch of holly. It filled the air with the familiar scent of pine.

Poof!

Peering down, Tim saw iron braces around his legs. Immediately, his limbs went all wobbly.

"You asked for your old self!"

Staring at his crippled legs, he asked, "Why don't I have a good body?"

"Who says your body isn't good?"

He pointed at his legs. "Can't you see the braces? I need a crutch to walk, and I feel weak and achy all the time."

Angel scanned his body from head to toe. "Hmm. It's your dream."

"But in real life, I'm a cripple."

"You don't love how you were created?"

"No!" he argued. "Would you?"

"Ah, now that brings me to what I'm here to show you. You wanted the experience of being human. Why you have your body at this time is not for me to say. But what I can say is that when you dropped down to

Earth, you forgot who you are — a beautiful soul born out of love. And in your forgetfulness, you came to believe, as most in your time, that you're just a body."

Tim's withered arms crossed around his chest. Even in his dream, his body felt real. "If I'm a soul, why did I come back with broken legs?"

"Ah, now *that* is a good question. The answer is found in the past." She twirled around and swished the branch of holly as if it was a magic wand.

Poof!

"This is Home."

Peering around, Tim saw no furniture, kitchen, or fireplace, only bright yellow light. "This isn't my home."

"Home is where you remember who you really are — a child of God." She rubbed her chin. "Hmm. Let's try another image." She struck the air with the holly.

Poof!

The two of them were transported to a golden cathedral with an immense sparkling dome. "This doesn't really exist," said Angel. "I'm imagining something that helps you understand the past."

Large golden doors to the cathedral opened as if they were beckoning arms. Entering, Tim found a pulsating sun in the dome of the roof showering particles of light that transformed into translucent orbs. They hovered around the room as if they were bright soap bubbles.

"Ah-h-h," cooed Tim, his eyes wide as saucers. "They're so pretty, like the shiny Christmas ornaments in the toy shop."

He immediately felt a warm glow in his heart. That glow extended through his body causing his braces to fall away. His body became luminescent.

He patted his arm and legs which felt all tingly. He then peered at the spheres and asked, "What are they?"

Angel glowed. "They're souls preparing to bring Christmas Spirit down to Earth. What do you feel?"

Tim felt his heart bursting with goodness. And his shimmering body felt less broken and more whole. "Love?"

Her nodding head caused the bells in her hair to tinkle. "That's who you are." She pointed to the glowing orbs. "They're preparing for their journey."

"Where are they going?"

"Millions of souls, particles of love, descend every day to spread the Spirit of Christmas. Right now, they're increasing their light before they leave so they don't completely forget who they are. But even then, most have trouble remembering where they come from after they're shaped and colored as a human. It takes lots of reminders — wake-up calls — to jog the memory."

Mesmerized by the pulsating light orbs, Tim moved closer to a particular sphere that transformed into a blazing sun.

"Imagine taking a deep breath before plunging into a dark pool of water," said Angel. "That's kind of what it's doing. Taking in extra light before it descends." She pointed at the tiny sun captivating his attention. "Watch."

Poof! It disappeared.

"Now for some fun," she said, twirling with glee. She waved the holly again.

Poof!

The two of them found themselves in a bedroom.

A midwife tends an exhausted woman who screams with pain when she experiences another contraction. The midwife rinses a compress in cold water and applies it to the woman's forehead covered in sweat.

"'Tis not an easy one," says the midwife. "Ye've been at it for some time. I fear ye won't last much longer. Push when the next one comes."

During the next contraction, the woman screams, causing the bed to shake.

"Push!" beckons the midwife, also sweating.

Following instructions, the woman grunts and groans as she pushes down. A tiny head finally appears.

"Yer doin' fine. Another push."

Out pops a baby's head.

Another push. A child is born.

"Hooray!" cried Angel. "You made it!"

"That's me?" asked Tim staring at the tiny creature who begins to wail.

"Yup. That's you. In a body!"

"But where's the tiny sun?"

She giggled causing the twinkling bells in her hair to jiggle. "Inside you, silly."

"But I don't feel it."

"Ah, this is where it gets interesting," said Angel. "When you sprouted out of the family tree, you absorbed the beliefs and feelings of your parents and their ancestors. It takes heaps of effort to adopt a language, customs, beliefs, emotions, and sadly, plenty of fears. That's the way it works on Earth."

"But where's the bright sun?"

She tapped his chest with her branch. "The light exists inside of you, silly. But just as everyone else trying to survive, you had to learn how to be a human with senses, emotions, and heaps and heaps of thoughts."

"But I don't remember the light."

Angel sighed. "You got lost in the world. It's hard to feel the light when you're stuck in a body that feels like a block of ice."

"But why did I come into a broken body?"

"You don't remember why you were born?"

Tim felt the braces return and his limbs grow weak. "Not to be crippled."

"You don't love your body?"

"No! Would you?"

Angel scratched the frizzy buns on her head and scanned his frame. "Hmm. I'd find it v-e-e-r-r-y-y interesting. Life on Earth is a playground. But it's short." She demonstrated by snapping her fingers. "This quick."

"I don't wanna experience pain," huffed Tim. "I just wanna fix my body and be strong like other boys." He rubbed his thigh. "I'm tired of being bullied by Matthew and Sniffy."

"Have you ever picked on anyone?"

"Never."

Angel raised her black eyebrows. "Humans get to taste heaps of emotions — anger, fear, sadness, hope, joy, love, and heaps more. You learned how it feels to get bullied." She tapped him on the head with the branch. "You also learned about being a bully."

"What?" asked Tim now raising his eyebrows. "I am not a bully," he protested.

"Oh yes you are!" she countered. "You can be quite cruel to yourself."

Tim's face flushed red. "I-I am not."

"When your legs hurt, you get mad and say mean things to yourself, that you're a worthless cripple."

"Well, I feel like that," he acknowledged.

"And then you bully yourself with dreadful thoughts."

Sighing, Tim said, "I'll be happy when this life is over."

The young girl rubbed his shoulders to comfort him. "Before it's over, let's find out why you're here." She pointed to the scene in the background where Tim's mother was nestling him as a newborn against her bosom. "When your mother became pregnant, she was anxious. She had already lost three, and she feared losing another baby. She passed that fear down to you."

"Fear?"

"As you grew inside her, you took on her feelings. The good and the bad. Fear became part of you. You forgot about your soul and came to believe that the light was somewhere up in heaven."

She pointed her branch upwards. "Heaven isn't up." She tapped Tim's chest with the holly, emitting the scent of pine. "It's inside. But come. We must visit another past."

"But—"

Poof!

He and Angel were immediately transported into a doctor's office. There, a man spoke with his father.

"Your son suffers from many maladies including rickets," says the man dressed in a black coat.

"Is there any hope for my son?"

The doctor shrugs. "Many children suffer from such maladies. With better food, medicines, sunshine, and fresh air, your son would have a better chance of surviving."

"But I can hardly afford bread and potatoes."

"London's winter does his lungs no good," says the doctor shaking his head. He opens the door to his office. "I wish there was more I could tell you."

His father leaves the office with tears streaming down his face.

"Why show me this?" asked Tim, wiping tears from his cheeks. He hated seeing his poor father suffer.

Angel's face morphed into a puzzled expression. "You don't know why I'm showing you this?"

The young boy shook his head.

"To help you see why you have this life. Experiences are neither good nor bad. They're just experiences. You can see a weakened body as a curse or as a blessing. Hardships bring pain but also gifts. I'm here to help you discover them."

He stamped a foot on the misty ground. "I feel pain every day. That's no gift."

"Suffering is painful," acknowledged Angel. "It's a natural part of being human. But the greatest suffering is the pain of thinking you're alone. That suffering can open a door where the light enters. That light connects you with your soul where you feel love and compassion."

She tapped Tim on the shoulder with her branch. "Do you not feel your father's pain when he comes home from work, his shoulders bent? He hates working for Scrooge."

"I worry about him."

"And he worries about you. Compassion is a gift. It shines light on another's soul. Remember the beggar by the toy shop?"

Nodding, he recalled the man who was now wearing his scarf.

"Because of the pain in your life, you felt his suffering, forgetting about your own discomfort. You extended love and, in doing so, helped him remember his inner light."

"Can't I do that without a crippled body?"

"Your limbs make it hard to get around and your body hurts, right?"

He nodded again.

"That opened you to the dreamworld — and me," she said proudly.

Before Tim could ask another question, Angel waved the holly. "Before my time is up, we must visit another past."

Poof!

A dinner scene appeared where Tim was a few years younger than his current self. He sat at the table on a stool next to his father on his left. To his right, his brother, Matthew, frowned, his face scrunched like a prune.

"Again?" complains his brother.

His mother dishes out a potato on his plate. "Be grateful we have food."

"But potatoes again?"

"'Tis been a lean year," interrupts his father. "Tiny Tim needed braces."

"Grrr," grumbles Matthew. He kicks Tim's foot under the table.

"Ouch," cries Tim.

"Matthew!" scolds his mother. "Go to yer room."

"Why am I always gettin' into trouble?"

"If you act like a bully, you get into trouble," answers his father. "Do as your mother says."

Matthew pushes his chair back in a huff and storms into the bedroom.

The scene shifts to the evening with Tim placing his crutch by the side of the bed and crawling under the blanket.

Matthew elbows him in the ribs and sneers, "That's for gettin' me in trouble."

Pain ripples down Tim's body. He whimpers but says nothing.

His brother whispers, "The only thing you're good at is makin' people feel sorry for ya. I don't feel sorry." He elbows Tim again.

"Cut it out," hisses Peter. The older brother pushes Matthew to the opposite side of the bed and takes up the middle. "Because of you, I must sleep in the middle again." He shoves him to the end of the cramped bed. "Don't hurt Tiny Tim."

"Grrr," grumbles Matthew. He pulls the blanket off his two brothers.

"Cut it out," shouts Peter.

He was always getting into trouble," said Tim. "It was better to say nothing when he hit me."

"Your mother had her hands full with six children," said the girl. "And with Matthew's temper, you tried to avoid fights. Following your father's example, you kept pain to yourself and acted nice to make it easier on everyone. But that made your body ache more. And when you suffered, others treated you with sympathy."

"My father took me to the doctor, but that cost money we didn't have. After a doctor's visit, we ate potatoes for two weeks."

"You chose to suffer so your family would not."

"Was better that way."

Angel tapped Tim with her holly. "But you suffered in silence."

He gazed at the apparition and mused, "Dreaming feels better than being in the real world."

"Who says this isn't the real world?"

"Because when I'm awake, you're not there."

"You think you're awake when you're really sleeping through life," she said. "That's why I'm here. To reveal the light of love. You're meant to shine it wherever you go and with whomever you're with."

"That's hard to do when my body hurts all the time."

Angel twirled the holly in her hand. The scent of pine wafted toward Tim. "I have a gift. Close your eyes and open your hands."

Tim did as he was told and extended his palms. Something heavy rested on them. Opening his eyes, he found three gold keys. He eyes widened. "What are these for?"

"You've heard about the keys to the kingdom of heaven?"

He nodded.

"These keys unlock memories of the past so you can embrace your real Home. Try one."

Tim chose a stubby gold key.

"That one unlocks the Power of Forgiveness. Insert it into your belly button."

The thought of sticking a key in a belly would have seemed ludicrous, but since anything could happen in a dream, Tim followed Angel's instructions. When he put the key into his navel, a horrifying image materialized — one that appeared in his nightmares. His belly morphed into a dingy, smelly prison cell with rusting bars. Terrified, he heard a grumbling, groaning sound that sent shivers up his spine.

Monsters! Evil creatures lurking inside the prison, screaming to eat his limbs. His body shook.

The girl placed a hand on Tim's shoulder. "It's not real. It's only your thoughts. They create the prison."

She guided Tim's shaking hand to turn the key. It disappeared into his navel. The door to the prison groaned then swung open. Black sludge poured out. Tim watched in horror as slimy, smelly sludge morphed into evil monsters. Some blazed with fiery eyes; others opened gaping mouths with piercing sharp teeth. Desperate to close the prison door, Tim pushed at the door, but the oncoming sludge forced it open.

"Help!" pleaded Tim, gazing at the outflow of monsters. He gagged at the stinky mess.

"That prison is where you stuff your feelings."

"What feelings?" he cried, battling to close the door.

"Resentment, fear, and anything from the past that makes you feel bad."

Tim sniffed and scowled. "They stink."

"Stinky thinky! You hold grudges."

Tim screamed, "Help!" A monster with pointed sharp teeth chomped on one of his legs and another one with fiery eyes clawed at his other leg.

Angel casually waved her branch of holly releasing red sparks and the familiar hint of pine. The monsters immediately stopped. "See how your grudges eat at you."

The young boy gazed at the image of Matthew in bed and felt the sludge of resentment he held inside. Not wanting to cause problems, he buried his anger, but he hated being bullied — by Matthew or Billy Pecksniff. And he hated his crippled body.

"You begrudge your body the most."

"It doesn't work like it's supposed to," whined Tim. "I wanna be like a normal boy."

"What is normal?"

"You know, with arms and legs that work. I wanna run and throw a ball." He kicked at the ground — not that there was any ground to kick in the dream world.

"Your body doesn't serve you?"

"You know the answer."

She fluffed out the ruffles on her red dress, then rearranged the evergreen garlands. "Do you love my dress?" she asked.

Confused by the abrupt question, Tim eyed the young girl. He did like the way she dressed, particularly the tinkling bells in her frizzy hair.

Reading his mind, she giggled. "I added jingle bells for a festive touch." She then poked him with her branch. "You chose a human form that serves you perfectly."

"Well, I pray for another body," he huffed.

"And what would you do with it?"

"What most boys do."

"You mean forget about your soul?"

Tim protested, "I wouldn't forget."

"Sniffy's body works, doesn't it?"

"Yeah."

"And he has money. Yet he uses his gifts to bully others. Now that doesn't say money or a body stops anyone from remembering the inner light. You can use money or your arms and legs however you choose."

Tim stared down at the prison in his belly. "I don't wanna have monsters."

"Your body doesn't cause monsters, your mind does. When you stuff painful feelings inside, you create sludge monsters."

"What should I do?"

"Release the monsters, silly!"

"What!" he exclaimed. "That's crazy!"

The young girl nodded, causing the bells in her hair to tinkle. "To some, it's crazy. But the key to letting go is to first welcome feelings when they appear. You can't be free until you see what you're stuffing. And if you can't see what you're stuffing, you can't let the feelings go."

Angel's hand reached out to Tim's belly. "Breathe in acceptance. Forgive yourself for being afraid. That happens when you're in a body."

Reluctantly, he took a deep breath.

"That's it. Welcome what's there. Be grateful for your feelings. They help you experience the world. Then breathe out what you no longer want."

Exhaling, Tim felt his body relax. With each breath, he felt a wave of peace.

"Good. Thank the sludge monsters for showing you anger." She pointed the holly toward one of the two remaining keys clutched tight in Tim's hand. "That one will help you release them."

The young boy fingered an ornate gold key with an engraved heart. He felt a rush of warm air flow into his chest.

"That unlocks the Power of Love."

"Where do I put it?"

"In your heart, silly."

Doing as instructed, he cautiously moved the key toward his chest. A red heart materialized. He gently placed the key in the center of the heart. It sprang open. A wave of love washed over him. It flowed into the prison cell, flushing out anger, resentment, and fear. The sludge monsters and the prison faded then disappeared.

Angel placed her hand on his heart. "The greatest key is love. Can you feel it?"

Nodding, Tim closed his eyes. "I do."

"Love yourself, no matter what, even when you're in pain. When you love yourself, you can love others." The young girl pointed the branch at Matthew who was fidgeting in bed and grumbling. "You have the key. Open his heart."

Overcome with love, Tim stared at his brother. He removed the key from his heart and pressed it against Matthew's chest. A red heart appeared and creaked open.

Immediately, Matthew relaxed in bed. His breathing entered a gentle calm rhythm. A smile emerged on his face.

"Your brother felt your loving kindness."

Tim pressed his hand against his own heart and felt compassion for his brother, realizing that Matthew's angry outbursts brought attention but also scorn. Gazing at him in bed, Tim sensed Matthew's pain about feeling unwanted and unloved.

"Feeling unloved is worse than physical pain. Your legs hurt, but you know your family cares for you. Matthew doesn't think so. He holds his pain inside his heart and takes it out on you. But you can help him."

"How?"

"By changing how you see him."

"What?"

Angel pointed to the final gold key. "Place that one on your forehead."

Tim inserted a long, slender gold key near his forehead. A keyhole immediately appeared and swallowed the key. *Click. Clack. Click. Clack.* The clicking and clacking sounded as if locks were opening.

Hopping with delight, Angel said, "You're unlocking the Power of Wisdom. The past offers wisdom when you learn from your experiences."

She waved her branch around his head. "Become one with the Supreme Light. See with the mind of God! Know where you came from and why you dropped down to Earth."

Tim flashed to the golden cathedral and the pulsating sun in the dome of the roof, transforming particles of light into shiny orbs. He was one of them.

"See everyone as suns of God who came to Earth for a taste of humanity."

Blinking his eyes, he stared at the yellow glow surrounding his brother's body."

"You're seeing the Christmas light!" said Angel, leaping with joy.

"Is that really Matthew?"

She was about to answer when the ruffles on her red dress shimmered and the bells in her hair tinkled and twinkled. "Oh, oh. Time to go. You have another visitor." She waved her holly. "Never forget who you are. Forgive, love, and see with the eyes of God."

With a broad smile and a final wave of her holly, Angel faded from view.

Chapter Three
The Second Spirit

Once again, Tim was alone in his dream. He assumed the visions would fade after he woke up: at least, that's how his dreams had worked in the past. He might remember a snippet here, a snippet there, but the whole dream would eventually be forgotten as a figment of his imagination.

Waiting for his next visitor, Tim twitched and turned in the bed.

Pop!

The popping sound in his head caused his eyes under closed eyelids to search for the noise in the dream. He found a laughing, plump, olive-skinned boy who was about his age. Dressed in an oversize green velvet robe with collar and sleeves trimmed in white fur, the boy wore a green bow tie made of holly and dotted with red berries. On his curly brown hair, a wreath of holly slipped over his blue eyes.

He pushed the wreath back on his head and announced himself. "Noel's the name." He laughed. "Actually, I'm the first Noel." He rubbed his round belly, then bowed. "The Spirit of Christmas Present at your service."

Tim stared wide-eyed at the apparition and sniffed the aroma of gingerbread. *If only I could live forever in my dreams*, he thought.

"Dreams do come true," chuckled Noel, reading his mind. He pushed back his overhanging green sleeves trimmed in white fur. "I have pressies for you. How about food?"

He clapped his hands. *Pop*! A Christmas cake and plum pudding materialized along with mince pie, sugar plums, juicy oranges, cherry-cheeked apples, roasted turkey, and a loaf of gingerbread.

Noel yanked a portion of gingerbread and stuffed it into his mouth. "Mmmm." He smacked his lips as the scent of gingerbread wafted in the air. Plucking a sugar plum, he tossed that into his gaping mouth revealing white, pearly teeth. He patted his belly and faced Tim. "Have some."

His mouth watering, even in a dream, Tim reached for a sugar plum. *Pop*! It disappeared.

"Wh-what happened?" he asked, confused and angry that it was whisked away.

Noel returned the slipping wreath back to the top of his head. His eyes flickered with mischief. "It's your dream," he said. "Try again. This time imagine something delicious and *really* desire it." Noel clapped his hands. "Whatever Tim desires, so shall it be!"

Pop! In front of Tim appeared a steaming cup of hot chocolate. He was about to reach for it when Noel held up his hands.

"Are you sure you want it?"

Since it was *his* dream, Tim readily nodded. Who wouldn't want hot chocolate on a wintry day?

Magically, the cup moved across the air toward him. Before it could disappear, he snatched it and took a sip.

"Good?" asked Noel.

The boy scowled. "I can't taste anything."

The Spirit conjured up a cup of chocolate for himself and drank it until it was empty. "Mmmm. Mine has a gingerbread taste—just as I ordered." He laughed. "How do you want yours to taste?"

"Chocolate, of course!"

"Then *really* imagine it."

A memory flashed to Tim—of the time when his father took him out for his birthday and bought him the most delicious cup of hot chocolate. As he imagined savoring each sip, his mouth drooled.

Noel's eyes sparkled. "You're getting the hang of it," he said. "Desire and enjoy!"

When Tim took another sip, he tasted heavenly chocolate. Fearing it would disappear, he quickly emptied the cup. Burping, he patted his stomach.

"I think you're ready for more Christmas pressies!" exclaimed Noel.

The thought of gifts thrilled the young boy. Since he had mostly received hand-me-downs, he nodded with excitement. His tongue swiped his lips for traces of chocolate.

"There's pressies every moment of the day," laughed Noel. "Nothing's permanent on Earth, just as in your dreams, but the Spirit of Christmas is ever-present."

"Christmas only comes once a year," corrected Tim.

Noel laughed so hard his belly jiggled. "Ha! Ha! You're funny!"

"There's only one December twenty-fifth," he said smugly.

"On *your* calendar. After the pressies are gone," he groaned, "everyone forgets about Christmas."

He clapped his hands. *Pop!* Another loaf of gingerbread appeared in front of him. He leaned over and inhaled its aroma. "Don't you love that smell?" Noel broke off a piece and ate it. "Mmmm. If you could eat something you love every day, wouldn't you get it?"

"The thought of eating food I loved *every day* would be like, well, celebrating Christmas every day!

"Exactly!" said Noel. He gleefully rubbed his hands. "Are you ready for pressies?"

Filled with anticipation, the young boy nodded. Who wouldn't want presents, even if they happened in the dream world?

Noel pushed back his green sleeves and lifted the wreath to its proper place. He clapped his hands once again. *Pop!* Four elaborately decorated boxes appeared.

"Oh, goodie!" he exclaimed. "Which one do you want to open first?"

The biggest box, half the size of Tim, was wrapped in silver paper and encircled with a shiny gold ribbon. Since that drew his immediate attention, he pointed at it.

"Touch the bow."

As soon as Tim touched the ribbon, the walls of the box fell away, and a scene unfolded before him. He saw his mother and sisters bustling in the kitchen.

Wearing a white kerchief over her head and an apron, now lightly soiled, over her grey dress, his mother prepares onion and sage stuffing. She chats with the second eldest daughter Belinda busily collecting ingredients for the Christmas pudding. Four years younger than her sister, Lucy peels potatoes.

"I worry so about Tiny Tim," says Belinda, wearing an apron smudged with flour.

"Shhh," whispers her mother. She nods toward Lucy.

Belinda takes the knife from her sister and says, "Go check on the boys. You can help them string the berries for the tree or make ornaments."

Delighted at the chance to cut out paper ornaments instead of peeling potatoes, the eight-year-old girl gladly darts into the other room.

"He's napping again," whispers Belinda. "He's getting weaker, have you noticed?"

Her mother nods. "I fret so. I don't know how many Christmas meals we'll have with Tiny Tim. I want this one to be special… in case…" Tears stream down her cheeks.

"Isn't there anything we can do?" asks Belinda, wiping her own tears.

Her mother pulls her to a corner of the kitchen so the children in the other room don't hear. "We're behind on our bills. We have no money for doctors."

"I can ask if Mrs. Jingle needs another maid," says Belinda.

Wiping her eyes, Emily Cratchit hugs her daughter. "Yer already helping us out by washing clothes for Mrs. Bell. If it weren't for ye and yer sister, we would be further behind in our bills."

As tears trickle down her mother's cheek, Belinda puts an arm around her. "Let's make this Christmas extra special. For Tiny Tim and Father."

"I fret about them." Her mother sighs. "Both put on a brave face, but I see the pain in their eyes."

"They're not letting me hang ornaments," grumbles Lucy storming into the kitchen. "Peter tells me we got to wait till Tim wakes up. I wanna hang them now!"

"Let them be," sniffles her mother. "Come, help me with the dressing."

Lucy stares at her mother's face. "Are you crying?"

"It's the onions, dear." She hands Lucy a wooden spoon. "Mix the stuffing."

The scene faded and the walls of the box refastened themselves in silver paper with the gold ribbon.

Tim blinked back tears. "If I wasn't alive, my parents would have more money."

"But they wouldn't have you, would they?" asked Noel. "Would you deprive them of miracles?"

"What miracles?"

The Spirit tapped Tim's shoulder. "Don't you remember what Angel showed you? That you're a soul pretending to be human?"

Tim pointed to his crippled legs. "This isn't pretend when I'm awake."

"When you're truly awake, you never ignore the presence of love." Noel pointed toward a green circular object in the shape of a hat box decorated with a cream lace bow. "Open that. You'll see what I mean."

After seeing his mother's tears, Tim wasn't so sure about opening another gift. He hesitated a moment, then reached for it. Upon his touch, the sides of the box dropped away, and a scene emerged.

Scrooge places coins in a drawer and locks it. "I have one more debt to collect," he announces to Bob Cratchit. "Another idle man spends my money. I will give him a Christmas present he will never forget."

"What will that be, Mr. Scrooge?" asks Tim's father, getting up from his desk.

His employer walks toward the door. "The last time, the scoundrel begged for mercy." He cackles. "I showed him mercy and charged him double interest. Now, I'll take possession of his house."

Horrified, Tim's father pleads, "Can it not wait, Mr. Scrooge? 'Tis Christmas."

"Bah! Humbug! I don't run a charity." He eyes his clerk with contempt. "Having you work for me is charity enough! Don't leave until you've finished all your work. Otherwise, I'll dock you the full day."

Tim's father nervously hands the coldhearted man his coat and top hat. "I hope it won't be too much trouble, Mr. Scrooge, if I have Christmas off."

"Every Christmas Eve, you ask the same," he sneers. "Why should I pay you for work you've never done?"

"Because it's Christmas?" asks his clerk meekly.

"Bah! Humbug!" shouts Scrooge. "It means nothing to me, except unearned wages."

"I-I'll complete all the paperwork before I leave," stammers Bob Cratchit. He offers Scrooge his scarf.

Snatching the scarf, Scrooge wraps it around his neck. "See that you do," he growls. "And come to work extra early the day after Christmas."

Hard as flint, Scrooge opens the door and steps out of the counting house and into the freezing air, muttering, "Bah, humbug. Christmas!"

Tim's father breathes a sigh of relief. He places a lump of coal on the fireplace and returns to his desk where he warms his hands over the candle. "Sorry, Tiny Tim," he mutters to himself. "I won't be home till late."

He rubs his eyes and stares at the stack of papers in front of him. Nestling into his tattered coat, he picks up the quill and copies figures into a ledger.

Tim watched in awe as the box magically rewrapped the scene back into the hat box with green paper topped with the lace bow.

"My father doesn't talk much of Mr. Scrooge," said Tim, shaking his weary head. "He's worked twenty years for him. He suffers so but says little."

"Like you," added Noel.

Tim winced. "Are you here to bring pain?"

"Pain? No, no, no. I'm here to bring miracles!"

"I don't see miracles. My father works for a cruel man."

"Is that what you see?"

Tim stamped his foot in the mist, but there was no sound. "If you can't see my father's pain, you're heartless."

Noel patted his chest, causing the red berries on his bow tie of holly to wiggle. "I don't have a physical heart." He pushed back his sleeves and straightened the bow tie. "But I see a miracle waiting to happen."

Tim scrunched his forehead. "What miracle?"

"The miracle of finding what's inside the pressies. Don't you love pressies?"

"Yeah... well... certain ones."

"When you unwrap them, you always find Christmas Presence." He pointed at the two other gifts. "Choose another."

Tim glanced at a yellow papered one with a purple bow, then at a dirty, striped-blue tube. He cringed at the thought of what might be inside since the other two previous presents revealed scenes he would rather not have watched.

"Everyone wants pressies to make them happy," laughed Noel, his belly jiggling. "Each moment is a gift begging to be unwrapped!"

He clapped his hand. *Pop*! Gingerbread materialized once more. He clapped his hands again. *Pop*! A pair of filthy shoes appeared. "Which one would you choose?"

Tim scrunched his face as if he was asked a crazy question. "Gingerbread, of course."

"Ah, but if your feet were bare, and there was snow on the ground, which would you choose then?"

"That's a trick question," answered the boy. "If I had no shoes, then any would be welcome."

"Exactly. You'd be excited to have warm feet."

"What does that have to do with Mr. Scrooge?"

"You see a nasty man; I see a lost soul who's forgotten who he is. Sooner or later, he'll find the light. Hopefully, while alive and if not, after death. The Spirit of Christmas is wrapped in a box of flesh and bones. Some wrappings dazzle; others repulse. Yet underneath, the light never goes out."

Noel picked up the dirty striped-blue cardboard tube. "Unwrapping pressies is fun when you have an open mind and heart. That's how you find miracles."

He handed the wrapped tube to Tim. "When Scrooge unwraps his life, he can discover generosity. Your father can find the power of love and even create abundance. And you… well, let's see what you uncover."

The young boy took the tube and tore at the striped-blue paper. It remained fastened shut.

"Ah," chuckled Noel. "This one you must touch with your heart. Hold it close to your chest."

When Tim nestled the tube against his chest, it burst open. Another scene unfolded.

A beggar with dirty rags for clothing wanders aimlessly down an icy street. Tim's woolen scarf marked with the letter T is wrapped around his neck and over the top of his head for warmth. When the beggar spots a man of means with a shiny black top hat and long coat made of fine wool, he hobbles toward him. "Kin ye spare a coin?"

The man scoffs at the beggar and shoves him to the gutter. "Be off." He wipes his gloved hands as if they had been sullied and walks past the beggar sprawled in the gutter.

"Let's unwrap that man," said Noel rubbing his hands together. "Gingerbread's my signature aroma. It reminds me of Christmas." He clapped. *Pop*!

The wealthy man halts and sniffs the air. He mumbles to himself, "Gingerbread?" He smiles. "Yes, gingerbread."

As if broken out of a trance, he glances back at the shabby beggar struggling to get up. He hurries to him. "My dear man, please forgive me. I have acted dreadfully. Let me help you."

The beggar warily eyes the wealthy man reaching out to him.

"I don't know what came over me," he says, shaking his head. He grabs an arm and lifts the

*poor man to his feet. "Forgive me, my dear man.
It's Christmas."*

*Eyeing the torn, dirty clothes, he reaches into
his pocket. "You're in sorry need of warm clothes
and a hearty meal." He hands the beggar a gold
sovereign. "Merry Christmas!"*

*The beggar's eyes widen. He takes the
sovereign and bites it to make sure it's real.
Shocked at finding the gold real, he says, "Thank
ye," still blinking in disbelief at the treasure in
his hand.*

The man tips his top hat. "Merry Christmas."

"How did you do that," asked Tim, forgetting that
in dreams anything could happen.

The Spirit gave a hearty laugh. "I helped the rich
man see beneath the rags and recognize a soul in
need. You did the same when you gave the beggar
your scarf."

Noel's wreath drooped over his eyes again. "My
time's getting short. You have another pressie to
unwrap." He lifted the wreath to sit properly on his
head, then pointed to a small box wrapped in yellow
paper with a purple bow.

Following Noel's instructions to connect with his
heart, Tim hugged the present to his chest. A scene
immediately appeared out of the box.

*Inside a lavish living room, Billy Pecksniff
awkwardly stands before his father and stares at
the floor.*

"Scrooge's nephew visited me," berates his father sitting behind a desk. "He told me what happened with the Cratchits. When Scrooge dies, and I hope it will be soon, Fred will take over the greedy miser's firm. I want their business so I must be on good terms with the nephew."

He stands up and, reaching across the desk, smacks Billy in the face. "That's for picking on a cripple where everyone can see. You made me look foolish. Don't ever embarrass me again."

Rubbing his cheek, Billy protests, "Ya tole me the Cratchits were scum. Was just 'avin' fun."

His father lifts his hand as a warning. "Don't embarrass me. I have a reputation to keep. Do as you wish with your friends but make sure no one sees what you do. Leave now. I have work to do."

Billy storms out of his house and collects his three cronies. Together, they skulk down a smelly side street. There they spot the beggar wearing Tim's scarf and a new coat, gobbling a meat pie.

The twelve-year-old boy checks up and down the street. Not seeing anyone, he rushes the beggar and knocks the meat pie out of his hands. "Lazy oaf!"

The four lads guffaw at the sight of the man scrabbling on the ground, picking up remnants of meat pie.

One of them kicks at the food and laughs. "Haw, Haw."

"Clap your hands," yelled Tim frantically. "Make them stop!"

"It's your turn," said Noel. He nodded toward them. "Send some love."

"They deserve a kick in the pants, not love."

"True," nodded the Spirit. "Kick them with love. No one really cares for Billy. His friends, if you could call them that, put up with him because his father has money. Kick him some love."

"How?"

"Why not sing 'The First Noel?' My favorite carol!" he exclaimed. "You can unwrap love by singing praises to our heavenly Lord."

When Tim thought of the way Billy treated him, resentment, not love, coursed through his body. He flashed to the memory of being called "Crutchit."

"You resent the outside wrapping," said Noel. "Try and see him as a Christmas pressie begging to be opened. Love what's on the inside."

"But how? You can clap your hands and make gingerbread."

"If you don't want to sing, then rub your hands together and shower him with a prayer such as, 'God bless you, Billy'."

Not quite ready to bless the lout, Tim rubbed his hands and modified the prayer. "God bless everyone."

"Now say it as if you really want to unwrap Billy and see the light."

A light inside a bully?! thought Tim.

Noel chuckled. "You know the answer. Each time you spread words of love, you create a miracle."

"Alright," grumbled Tim. "I still think he deserves a kick in the pants, and then some."

Noel laughed and his belly jiggled. "You're a stubborn one, aren't you?" The plump olive-skinned boy tugged at his oversize green velvet robe. "Be careful what you wish for. Haven't you heard the saying, 'As you sow, so shall you reap?' If you send Billy a kick in the pants, he'll return the favor."

Tim glared at the Spirit's blue eyes. "I don't have your powers."

After lifting the slipping wreath of holly back over his head, Noel pulled the sleeves back and clapped his hands. *Pop*! The scent of gingerbread filled the air. "What am I holding?"

"Gingerbread."

"Right you are." Pieces of gingerbread rested in his palms. "Imagine gingerbread; it appears. Miracles work the same way. Look for love; that's what you'll find. Try that with Billy."

Tim took a deep breath and rubbed his hands fervently. He took another deep breath and exhaled. "God bless you."

Nothing happened.

"Say it again. Really feel love and, for good measure, toss in a 'Merry Christmas'."

The young boy shook his body to release the resentment. He then closed his eyes and pictured his father's love. His heart swelled. "May God bless you, Billy. Merry Christmas."

Then he saw Billy's nose sniff the air.

"Can you smell chocolate?" he asks his cronies.

The three lads sniff and nod. A brawny one says, "Oy. I smell somethin' like that."

They check down the street, looking for the source of the tantalizing aroma but see nothing.

Noticing the beggar on his knees grasping for the scraps of food, Billy's face reddens. He sniffs the aroma of chocolate and turns to his three companions, "Let's help him."

"Wha?" asks the brawny one but after he inhales another whiff of chocolate, says, "Yeah, right." He helps Billy lift the man up and brush off his new coat.

Reaching into his pocket, Billy retrieves an apple and a coin. He hands them to the beggar and says, "Sorry, sir."

Being called "sir" stuns the poor man as well as the three cronies who never heard Billy apologize for anything.

The beggar clutches the apple and coin in his hand and stares at the four boys. "'Tis a strange Christmas, lads." His spare hand clutches the scarf on his new coat. "Angels are about."

Noel heartily patted Tim on his shoulder. "Oh, goodie! Your love for chocolate created a miracle. Must be your signature aroma. Let it remind you to create more miracles. Just see everyone, including yourself, as pressies begging to be unwrapped."

Noel paused and rubbed his belly. "Someone should write a song and proclaim, 'All you need is love'." He laughed heartily. "Would make a wonderful song."

He cocked his head as if hearing something. "The Spirit of Christmas Future seeks your company." He took the wreath off his head and bowed. As he vanished, he whispered, "All you need is…"

Chapter Four
The Third Spirit

For a brief time, Tim remained alone in his dream world. *Such magical Spirits,* he thought. And with one Spirit yet to come, he was bursting with anticipation, like any child waiting for Christmas.

Whoosh! Before him stood a young girl with short violet hair, at least, that's what he first saw. The hair began growing to shoulder length. Then the violet hair grew shorter on the left side of her head while the hair on the right side slipped well below her shoulders.

"I don't know what to do with my hair," said the petite girl in a flowing lavender dress dotted with amethyst crystals. Her face with brown almond eyes reminded Tim of the Orient.

"Are you the Spirit of Christmas Future?" he asked.

The girl blew into a small torch and ignited a flame. "I'm El, short for Uriella. Means God's light." Wisps of smoke that smelled like church incense curled upward. She waved the torch around her head and the lengthening and shortening of her straight hair stopped.

"So many choices," she said. "Which way looks better? Do I look prettier with long or short hair?"

Tim blushed because she looked pretty no matter the cut of her hair.

"That's what I thought," she said. "Do you want me to give your hair a new color?" Before he could reply, she waved the torch over his head.

Whoosh! His hair turned red with green and white stripes.

"Don't care for the stripes," she mused. "But you need a Christmassy look. How about this?"

She waved the torch again. *Whoosh*! A star rested on top of his head with his hair now bright green. "Yes!" She materialized a mirror and showed him the new look.

Tim recoiled at the sight and gasped, "I look like a Christmas tree! Please turn it back to the way it was."

El shrugged. "If you choose bad hair, so be it."

She moved the torch over his head again. *Whoosh*! The unruly mop of brown hair returned.

"Feel better?"

Seeing himself in the mirror, he breathed a sigh of relief. "More like my old self."

"You've been complaining about your old self for a long time. Bad legs, bad arms, bad body. And if you ask me, I'd say bad hair. And when I brought more color to your life, what did you choose? Same old, same old. Boring!"

"I'm used to the way I am."

"Are you happy with what you see?"

"No, but I was born this way."

"And you want to keep it that way!" She blew into the torch again, sending fragrant smoke into the air. "Smell the frankincense," she said. "I got it from one of the three wise men while they followed the star. Speaking of stars, do you want to reach for one?"

"What do you mean?"

"You have a choice about what may come."

Tim pointed to the iron braces on his legs and his withered arms. "I'm stuck with these."

The young girl shook her head. "Even in this dream, you're sticking with what you know. I offered Christmassy hair, and you chose bad hair."

Tim pressed his hand over his head. "My hair's not bad."

The Spirit rolled her eyes. "If you think so!" She lifted the torch near her head. *Whoosh!* The violet shade turned shocking pink, and the hair fell to her waist. She admired herself in the mirror, then tossed it into the air where it vanished. "In the dream world, you can imagine what you desire and make them come true. What you choose affects your future. I'm here to light the way of what may be."

She blew into the torch. *Whoosh!*

A stately drawing room with lavish furnishings materializes. Paintings of angels hang on the walls. A roaring fire blazes while a young woman plays a Christmas carol on a grand piano. An enormous Christmas tree occupies the center of the room.

A few of Tim's siblings, now five years older, are decorating the tree with candles and red and green baubles. A fit eleven-year-old boy stands on a ladder and places a star on the top of the tree.

"Nice work, Tim," says his brother, Matthew. "Without the braces, your legs are getting stronger."

His father, dressed in exquisite clothes, promenades into the room with his mother dressed in a flowing red dress. They bring Christmas punch and a plate of delectable sweets into the room. Tim's sister, Belinda, plays "Joy to the World."

Tim climbs down from the ladder. He grabs a glass of punch and a sugar biscuit, then joins the others around the piano, singing "Joy to the World…"

"Can this be?" asked Tim.

"Oh, this is but one of many futures," answered El. "The choice is yours."

"How can that be?" He pointed at his legs. "Can they get better?"

"That I cannot say. Much depends on the choices you and others make. Your choices depend on what you desire."

"What I desire is to be rid of the pain when I wake up from this dream."

"Do you mean the pain in your body or in your mind?"

"I only feel pain in my legs and arms," he said.

El cocked her head. "I see brain pain. You're ashamed of how you look and mad that you're not like other boys."

"I try to forget about that."

"Didn't the Spirit of Christmas Past show you what happens when you lock the pain inside?"

Tim rubbed his tummy where his bad feelings grumbled. "I wanna rid myself of those feelings as well."

"Then let's visit another place." The girl blew into the torch and sent sparks and frankincense smoke into the air. *Whoosh!*

The elegant room transforms into a bleak, frigid cemetery. Two gravestones loom from the earth.

The joyous feeling that Tim felt watching his family sing carols deflated like a balloon. His eyes focused on the writing engraved on one of the stones.

"No," he screamed. "My father!" He reached out to touch the tombstone, but his hands went through the phantom image.

His eyes veered to the other headstone and shrieked, "Me?!"

Checking the dates of death, he gasped. Tears ran down his cheeks. "I don't have long to live. Neither does my father."

Precious memories flashed into his mind of his father ruffling his brown hair, tenderly carrying him on his shoulder, and loving him just the way he was. Grief-stricken, Tim stared at the graves and wept. The thought of losing his beloved father, more so than his own life, made his body convulse with pain.

As tears streamed down his cheeks, Tim turned to the Spirit. "At first, you showed me a future filled with joy. This future brings only sorrow." He wept. "I can't bear this."

"You and your father are close," nodded El. "Close in life; close in death."

Tim wiped his eyes. "Why show me joy, then take it away?"

El furrowed her brow and stared at the young boy. "You can see sorrow, or you can see joy. The choice is yours."

Outraged by those words, Tim stamped his foot on the misty ground. "What choice?" He waved at the marked graves. "My father and I are dead."

"You can see sorrow, or you can see joy," repeated El. She waved her torch. *Whoosh*!

Immense doors opened to a golden cathedral, similar to the place where the Spirit of Christmas Past brought him.

"Let's go in," said El, leading the way.

Entering the cathedral, Tim found thousands of translucent orbs of light pulsating in the air. Little suns kept popping into the room. They floated around the cathedral before merging into an immense sun pulsating above in the dome.

Pointing to the sparkling spheres, El grinned. "Returning souls. They've completed their journey on Earth. They're happy to come back Home."

Just then an orb burst into the cathedral. The other globes glowed brightly to greet the ball of light.

"Hurrah!" beamed El. "Welcome Home!"

Tim grew quiet. "I died."

The Spirit seemed amused. "No one ever dies." She waved the torch over her head. *Whoosh*! Her hair color morphed from shocking pink to violet with the left side of her head cut short and the hair on the right side falling to her waist. "What do you think of the change?"

Unsure of what to say, he stared at the petite girl from the Orient.

"Your body's always changing — same as my hair. When you no longer need a body, you leave it and return back to who you really are — one with God."

Another orb popped into the cathedral, and again the entire room illuminated a grand welcome.

El clapped her hands. "Hurrah! Your father's joined the party."

Tim stared at the sunlike globe. As soon as it hovered near his right shoulder, he felt unconditional love.

Facing the sphere, he asked, "Father?"

The orb pulsated radiant light, swelling Tim's heart with love.

"It *is* you!"

The young boy's body tingled and shimmered. The sorrow that he felt in the cemetery washed away, making the pain seem tinier than a grain of sand on a vast beach.

"You're here to have lots of experiences. I'm here to remind you to choose the Spirit of Christmas."

Tim gazed at all the orbs popping into the cathedral. "Am I gonna die soon?"

"Your physical body ends when you're done living. Are you done living on Earth?"

Tim thought of his crippled legs. He wanted to be done with the horrible pain. But then he flashed to his family. His father would be devastated by his death.

"If I return, what is yet to come?" he asked.

She blew into the torch. The aroma of frankincense filled the air as her hair changed to gold, then to green, then back to violet. "Do you want to return as your old self with the same bad hair?"

The hair Tim did not mind. But the pain in his legs and arms he did not want. "Can I change that?" he asked, knowing El understood.

She thought for a moment, then answered, "Think of your body as the wax in a candle. When the wick is lit, the wax melts. When the wax is all used up, you'll be dying to return home and become one with the big candle. Death means you lose your waxy old self."

Raising her torch, the Spirit asked, "What shall it be? Remain here or return to Earth?"

"If I returned, I want it to be different."

She touched the top of Tim's head. "Get rid of the bad hair."

"You know what I mean. Can I have a future like the one I saw with my family around a piano, singing carols."

The amethyst stones on her dress sparkled as she leaned in close. "The future depends on what you choose. You can choose fear, or you can choose the

Spirit of Christmas where love guides you just as the star guided the three wise men. Those wise men carried gifts — gold, frankincense, and myrrh."

She raised the torch. "I offer you three Christmas wishes. The future reflects what you desire so before you choose, use your imagination. What do you long for?"

The young boy felt overwhelmed. Never before had he been offered three wishes that could change his future.

"And you can't wish for more wishes," she added with an impish smile. "That'd be cheating."

Glancing at his withered arms and legs, Tim answered, "I want a healthy body so I can get around without braces and a crutch."

Her eyes twinkled as she blew into the torch. A cloud of frankincense lifted into the air. *Whoosh!* Tim's body was immediately transformed into that of a healthy six-year-old boy — with long bright green hair.

Noticing the colored strands of hair drooping in front of his eyes, he protested, "I don't wanna look like this! Change it back."

"If that's what you want," answered El. She puffed into the torch. *Whoosh!* The green hair morphed back into his brown tousled mane, and his former crippled body returned. "That was your second wish."

"Hey," grumbled Tim. "I didn't wanna use another wish!"

The Spirit edged closer. "You wanted to feel healthy and already you're complaining. Just as most humans do! You want something, get it, then complain about what you don't have."

Tim scratched his head. "But this is a dream."

"A dream is more real than sleepwalking through life." Her eyes sparkled. "You can play with futures in the dream world just as we're doing, and you can do the same after you wake up. It all depends on your imagination and what you choose to believe."

"I can wish for anything?"

Her impish smile returned. "Be careful what you wish for. If you wish for a perfect body, you might get exactly what you have. You may not care for your weak legs and arms, but they may give you the perfect experience to learn about love."

"It's hard to feel love when I ache all over," he complained.

"When your body hurts, you can act this way or that way, you can look for something bad or something good, you can curse what you have, or you can bless it. Your mind is free to choose. Those choices create your future. Eventually, you'll share the same future as everyone else and return Home."

The young boy glanced at his crippled body. He wanted his final wish to be the best wish ever. Strong legs and arms would eliminate pain, and other boys wouldn't mock him. He then thought of the big house with the grand piano. Money would mean his father could stop working for Scrooge. Living in luxury surrounded by his family would be a future he would joyfully welcome.

"It's hard to decide!"

The Spirit seemed preoccupied with changing the color and shape of her hair again. "Maybe something. Gold lavender?"

"Please help me decide?" pleaded the boy.

With golden hair on one side and lavender strands on the other side, El tapped Tim's forehead. "Think with the mind of God. But before you decide, watch what happens when someone chooses one way and then another."

She blew into the torch, releasing more frankincense. *Whoosh!*

In a bleak tavern sits a solitary man scowling at a plate of cheese, overcooked beef, and a potato.

"Will ye be wantin' somethin' else?" asked the surly woman waiting on him.

He pokes a fork at the half-cooked potato. "You call this pig's dinner food?"

"The best we 'av on Christmas Eve. Finish up. We're closin' for the night. I 'ave wee little ones at home."

"Brats, you mean," gripes Scrooge. "Vermin. They cost money."

The woman winces. "I'll 'ave none a that." *She snarls, "Git, ya ole fool."*

"I paid good money for this... pig's dinner. I'll leave when I'm done."

The woman growls and leaves in a huff.

With an impish smile, El said, "Mr. Scrooge will meet some unexpected Spirits tonight."

"Will it be you, Angel, and Noel?"

She shook her gold and lavender hair. "Oh, no. He hates children. He needs Spirits who will make him pay attention and unwrap his life." Lifting her torch, she giggled. "Watch what happens when he comes to his senses." She blew into the flame. *Whoosh!* The scene changed.

In the evening on Christmas Day, the Cratchit family sits around the fireplace. A knock at the door causes everyone to jump.

"Who on earth would be coming at this hour?" asks Mrs. Cratchit.

Bob opens the door and finds Ebenezer Scrooge, his arms overflowing with packages.

"May I come in, Bob? I must relieve my arms of these burdens."

"Why, yes, of course."

Quite jubilant, Ebenezer places the packages on the table and gazes at the children's eyes that had grown as large as saucers.

"Ah, such lovely children. Delightful children," he remarks. "And this must be Tiny Tim." He bends over and gently ruffles his brown hair. "Lovely boy. I have something for you and for everyone. The shops were closed, but when I opened my purse, the shopkeepers were all too happy to open their doors."

He laughs heartily as he hands out packages wrapped in brown paper. Each child receives a present. Unwrapping his gift, Peter gasps at a chess set, and Belinda screams when she discovers music books. Martha beams at a sewing basket filled with needles and threads, and Matthew proudly bangs on a toy drum. Lucy burst into tears when she unwraps a doll with a frilly pink dress.

Tiny Tim waits until his siblings open their presents then unwraps his. His eyes gaze at the wooden box emblazoned with the word Thaumatrope.

"What's a Tomato…rope," he asks, struggling with the word.

Scrooge chuckles and pronounces the word correctly. "A thaumatrope creates an optical illusion." He giggles. "Open the box."

Tim's hands shake with excitement as he opens the container. Inside, he finds twelve cardboard discs with painted pictures. Each disc has strings attached, one to the left side of its picture and another to the right side.

"Go ahead," encourages Scrooge. "Pick one."

Tim chooses one of the discs. He stares at the picture of a yellow canary on one side, then turns it over to find a picture of an empty birdcage.

"Hold one string with your left fingers and the other string with your right fingers," instructs Scrooge. "Yes. That's it. Now twirl the disc."

With both hands, Tiny Tim spins the disc. His eyes widen. "Look! The bird is in the cage!"

The family oohs and ahhs.

He gasps. "How did that happen?"

"That's called an optical illusion," giggles Scrooge. "Try another."

This time Tim chooses a disc with a picture of red roses on one side and an empty vase on the other. When he twirls it, he creates a vase filled with roses.

That produces more **oohs** and **ahhs** from everyone.

Raising his eyes towards Scrooge, Tiny Tim blinks away tears. "God bless you, Mr. Scrooge."

Unsure what to make of the generous display, Emily nudges her dumbfounded husband.

"Oh, yes," he says to his children. "What do you say to Mr. Scrooge?"

In unison they yell, "Thank you, Mr. Scrooge!"

"Remarkable children," giggles Ebenezer. "Delightful children."

"And thank you for the prize turkey," says Bob. "The poulterer sent it early this morn."

"Oh, yes, Mr. Scrooge," adds Emily. "That was very generous of ye. We have plenty to share. Would ye have some?"

"Heavens, no." He pats his stomach. "I'm stuffed from my meal at Fred's house."

"You supped with your nephew?" asks Bob.

Ebenezer laughs. "I came to my senses, Bob. I was an old fool for refusing to meet his wife. She's a lovely woman." He shifts his gaze to Emily. "And you're a lucky man to have such a wonderful wife."

Emily blushes, not knowing what to say.

He points to a bottle on the table and tells her, "I thought you and your husband might enjoy some sherry."

Emily protests. "Ye've given more than enough, Mr. Scrooge. We can't take it."

"Nonsense," he says. "I should be giving you more." He ruffles the hair of each child clutching their gifts. "Remarkable children. Delightful children." He turns to Tiny Tim. "And we shall get you the best medical care."

Mesmerized by the scene, Tim asked, "What happened to him? Did he go mad?"

El laughed. "Heavens no. He came to his senses and chose love." She lifted her torch. "Your turn. What's your final wish?"

So many decisions, thought Tim. *A strong body, lots of money…?*

"Think of what you desire," said the Spirit, casually running fingers through her hair that had turned sapphire blue.

Closing his eyes, he focused on his heart. A body that worked would make him happy.

He paused a moment then opened his eyes. "I have my final Christmas wish."

The Spirit stopped stroking her hair, which had turned back to violet. "What shall it be?"

After taking a deep breath, Tim announced, "I wish to see the light in myself and in everyone."

Hearing that, the girl leapt with joy. "Hurrah! You chose the Spirit of Christmas—even if it meant keeping your body the way it is." She wrapped her arms around him. "Bless you for having the courage to act with a loving heart. You bring glad tidings of joy."

Her tender hug made Tim's body glow.

With the amethyst crystals shimmering on her dress, El waved the torch and sent sparks and smoke into the air. "Let the Child born in Bethlehem remind you that you are also a child of God. See through the eyes of love. Listen with the ears of love."

She blew into the flame a final time. "When two or more are gathered in the everlasting light, heaven sparkles with delight. Glory to God in the highest, and on Earth, peace and good will to all."

Whoosh! The girl disappeared and so did the dreamtime.

Chapter Five
The Awakening

"Time to wake up, my dear."

"Huh?" yawned Tim. He opened his eyes and saw his mother. He gasped. "Did I miss Christmas?!"

"No," she laughed. "It's nine o'clock on Christmas Eve. I came to wake ye earlier, but ye looked so peaceful in yer sleep."

"Christmas Spirits visited me in a dream," he gushed.

His mother smiled. "Glad ye had a good dream." She handed him his iron braces. "Help us prepare the house before yer father arrives."

With the memories of his dream fresh in his mind, Tim reached for the metal supports. His limbs seemed lighter, and he felt little pain. A smile creased his face. Even if his legs and arms ached, that wouldn't stop him from enjoying Christmas. He strapped on the braces and reached for his wooden crutch. Brimming with excitement, he yearned to share his wondrous dream but decided to save the details for when his father returned home.

He hobbled into the room where the fireplace warmed the air. Near the small window, Lucy decorated the spindly fir tree with paper ornaments while Matthew grumbled about stringing red berries for the tree. Peter, wearing his father's old shirt with an oversize collar, was hanging eight worn stockings near the fireplace.

Spotting Tim, Lucy rushed to him. "Mother told us to wait until you woke up," she said, "but you slept so long." She handed him three paper ornaments. "I saved these three for you to hang on the tree." She beamed. "I cut them out myself."

Tim stared wide-eyed at the cutouts in the shape of angels. He shuffled to the table where paper scraps, pencils, and scissors littered the surface. Grabbing a pencil, he wrote ANGEL on one, then placed it on a naked branch.

"Angel appeared in my dream," he said excitedly. "She showed me the light I have inside me."

Matthew and Lucy glanced at each other and shrugged believing Tim was in his imaginary world as he often was. However, Peter paused and sniffed the apples and chestnuts he was holding, ready to drop them into stockings. Confused, he said, "These smell like a Christmas tree."

Tim giggled. "That's pine—Angel's special fragrance."

His sister and two brothers gave each other furtive looks as they watched Tim return to the table.

After printing the name NOEL on another cutout, he placed it on another branch. "This one's for Noel. He told me to unwrap Christmas Presence every day."

Sniffing the air, Lucy asked, "Is Mother baking gingerbread?"

"That's Noel," said Tim now laughing. "He made gingerbread appear in my dream."

Before anyone could say anything, he grabbed the third paper ornament and printed the name EL. "The third Spirit El asked me to bless everyone with love." He nodded at Peter, Lucy, then Matthew. "We are all children of God."

The three of them stared at their brother, not knowing what to say. The silence was broken when Belinda burst into the room.

"When you're done with the decorations," she announced, "Mother and I need help in the kitchen. We want everything to be perfect when father arrives."

"He's always late," grumbled Matthew. "Evil Scrooge makes him work extra hard on Christmas Eve."

"Today, Scrooge will choose love," said Tim with a beguiling smile.

Before Matthew could reply with something mean, Peter told him, "You and Tim can finish hanging ornaments. Lucy and I will help in the kitchen." His face became stern as he admonished Matthew. "Don't cause trouble." He then left with Lucy and Belinda, hoping his brother would be on his best behavior.

But hoping wasn't good enough because as soon as Peter left the room, Matthew ripped the paper angels off the tree. "These are stupid," he barked. He tossed them to the floor and stomped on them.

Tears dropped from Tim's eyes as he stared at the decorations on the floor. He spotted the ornament with Angel's name printed on it and flashed to the Spirit of Christmas Past. Imagining the three gold keys that she had given him, he mentally inserted the stubby one into his stomach. He turned the key to the power of forgiveness. Immediately, he felt rumbling in his stomach—the place where he stored anger. He hated the way his brother treated him.

Normally, Tim would have cowered and said nothing. But this time, he forgave himself for having the feelings, even the urge to smack his brother's mouth with the crutch and give him another chipped tooth.

He paused, accepting that he was *very* mad, something he rarely let himself feel. Hobbling toward Matthew, he declared, "You're mean. And I don't like it." He wiped his eyes. "You hurt me, and I know why you do it."

Matthew tapped his own head and sneered, "You're soft up here like your bones."

"Stop it!"

His brother recoiled, dumbfounded. He never heard Tim speak harshly.

"You say mean things to get attention."

"Do not!"

Turning his gaze to the paper angels on the floor, Tim said, "You stomped on my feelings."

"Boo hoo," taunted his brother, recovering his swagger.

"I'm gonna forgive myself when I'm mad," announced Tim. "And I'm gonna forgive you 'cause you don't know who you are."

Stunned by those words, Matthew stared at his brother, who was acting so unlike himself.

"I wanna give you a present," said Tim, edging closer.

"You don't have money ta buy a present."

"Spirits gave me something money can't buy."

That caught Matthew's attention. "What're ya talkin' about."

Tim recalled the large gold key. Imagining his index finger becoming the key to love, he pointed it at Matthew's chest. "There's a light in there."

Confused, his brother glanced down at his shirt and scoffed, "Nothin's there."

Tim pressed his finger firmly against his brother's chest.

Matthew swiped it away. "You're crazy."

If you're a pressie, thought Tim, *you must have a light somewhere in there.* He pictured the third gold key accessing the power of wisdom and the mind of God. A yellow glow appeared around his brother.

"I see the light!" he beamed.

Matthew scowled at his brother. "You're—" He stopped midsentence. He sniffed the air and wiggled his nose. "Is mother making hot chocolate?"

Hearing this, Tim giggled. "Chocolate's my secret power."

His brother slowly inhaled through his nose. "Mmmm. I do smell chocolate." He nervously glanced around as if sensing the presence of an invisible force. Looking down, he spotted the paper ornaments on the floor. After hesitating a moment, he reached down and picked them up. Brushing them off, he placed them on the tree and muttered, "Sorry."

That one word, rarely uttered by Matthew, gave Tim an unexpected miracle.

By ten o'clock, the preparations were complete. Waiting for their father, the Cratchit children gathered around the fireplace.

"Shouldn't Father be home by now?" Tim asked his mother coming in from the kitchen.

She checked the wall clock. "Shouldn't be long, dear." She didn't want to say it, but she was worried about her husband and furious at Scrooge whose nasty temper proved vile during this festive time of the year. Bob had never worked past ten.

When the clock struck eleven, Emily Cratchit's nerves unsettled her. "Go see what's come of yer father, Peter."

Grabbing his coat and scarf, he reached for the door when it burst open.

Chuckling aloud, Bob yelled, "Merry Christmas!" He rushed to his family huddled near the fireplace and grabbed Emily. He hugged and kissed her as if he had not seen her in months.

"What's got over ye, Robert?" cried his red-faced wife. She nodded at the children. "They were worried. That horrid Scrooge. He's a beast of a man."

"'Tis Christmas, my dear," her husband chortled. "Even Mr. Scrooge deserves kindness. Besides, something marvelous has happened."

Overwhelmed with joy, he grabbed each child— Tiny Tim, Lucy, Belinda, Matthew, and Peter—and smothered them in hugs until they were all giggling and laughing.

Emily smelled her husband's breath. "Have ye been drinking, Robert Cratchit? Ye seem unlike yourself."

His face flushed. "I've had a brandy with Mr. Scrooge's nephew," he confessed. "But it's not the alcohol that brings me such merriment, my dear." He paused and looked toward the kitchen. "Where's Martha?"

"She's been putting in long hours at the milliner's shop," said Emily. "After work, she planned to drop off a present for a friend. She never misses Christmas dinner."

"I hope she comes home soon. But gather 'round, everyone."

His wife and children crowded around him, captivated by his excitement.

"I received a marvelous Christmas present." He raised his eyes upward as if acknowledging angelic visitors. "I was blessed by Spirits this holy day."

"So was I," cried Tim.

"There you have it," said Bob. "Christmas Spirits are everywhere." He put his arm around Tiny Tim. "We shall share our stories after we visit the church as we always do on Christmas Eve." He sniffed the air. "The bird smells delicious."

He sent his wife a loving smile. "No doubt, you have cooked the most splendid goose with onion and sage stuffing."

"Are ye right?" asked his wife, wondering what had come over her husband. He was usually cheerful about Christmas, but this time his eyes sparkled and his body glowed.

Bob kissed his wife. "My dear, I've never been so happy to be with my family." He glanced at the clock. "But it's getting late. Today is not one to break tradition. Tiny Tim and I must visit the church before midnight and pray for his health."

"Then off with ye," said Emily, pushing him towards the door. "The food shall be ready when ye return."

"And then I shall tell a miraculous story."

"As shall I," said Tim clapping his hands. "'Tis filled with miracles."

With a twinkle in his eyes, Bob laughed. "We both have much to tell." He exploded into a huge belly laugh. "So much to tell!"

"Tell us now," begged Peter, looking rather comical in his father's oversize collar.

"That will have to wait." He picked up Tiny Tim's crutch. "Come, lad." He hoisted his son off the ground, his limbs supported by an iron frame, and placed him on his shoulders.

"Hurry home," pressed his wife. She turned to the other children. "Come. I need ye in the kitchen."

While the children hurried after their mother, Tim, perched on his father's shoulder, giggled as his father walked briskly in the falling snow to the old stone church. There, other visitors gathered to pray before the night turned into Christmas morning.

Settling into a pew with his father, Tim sat motionless, watching the candles flicker on the altar. He pointed toward a stained-glass window and whispered, "Father, I see the Spirits who visited me in my dream."

Startled by his son's comment, Bob glanced at the scene depicting three angels hovering above a glowing manger. "The ones on the glass window?"

"No, they're floating above it." Tim sniffed the air. "I smell pine." He sniffed again. "Now gingerbread." Sniffing once more, he smiled. "Frankincense. The Spirits from my dream are here. They're so bright, my eyes are hurting."

Bob smelled similar scents. He marveled at what his son told him for he, too, had been visited by Christmas Spirits while at work. And each one brought scents similar to the ones described by Tim.

Tenderly placing an arm around his son, Bob whispered, "Miracles have occurred this wondrous night. Angels are here when we need them." He gently squeezed Tim's shoulder. "Let's ask them to shower our family with Christmas Spirit."

"If it wasn't for Christmas, the lame wouldn't walk, and the blind couldn't see," said Tim.

"Exactly!"

Father and son closed their eyes in prayer. Those in the church would later state that a glowing light surrounded the two praying in silence.

Bong. Bong. Bong....

When the church bells struck midnight, the two left the church. Sitting back on his father's shoulders, Tim gazed at the full moon illuminating the carpeted snow on the ground.

Approaching an icy patch, Bob skidded to give his son a thrill.

"Do it again," shouted Tim.

"We shan't be late for our Christmas meal," laughed Bob, but unable to contain his giddiness, he skidded several more times on the ice, screaming *wh-e-e-e* along with his son.

Filled with merriment, they arrived home to the smell of Christmas goose permeating the air. Four children immediately gathered around their father and helped Tiny Tim off his shoulders.

Bob glanced around. "Martha? Where's Martha? We must have our family together on this joyous feast."

When the other children started sniggering, Martha popped out from behind the closet door where she was hiding. "Surprise!"

Bob rushed to hug his eldest daughter. "God bless you, Martha." He hugged her again and again, filling his heart with delight.

"We have the best family in the world," beamed Tim.

"Indeed, we do," said Bob. "And I have the best wife ever."

Emily blushed. "Ye are in a rare mood, Bob Cratchit. Let's sit down before the meal gets cold."

Taking his place next to his father who sat at the head of the table, Tim widened his eyes as a parade of food landed on the table — the small baked goose with onion and sage stuffing, mashed potatoes and gravy, and sweet applesauce. That might not have been considered a feast for many, but to the family of eight who rarely left the table with full bellies, the meal represented heavenly abundance.

Before Bob picked up the knife to carve the bird, he asked everyone to hold hands and bow their heads to join in a silent prayer for those in need. After a moment, he joyously proclaimed, "Let's eat!"

Oh, such a clamor of knives and forks as plates were filled and emptied into hungry mouths! Nothing was left of the goose except bones that were picked clean.

Bob found the wishbone and handed it to Tim. "'Tis tradition for one to pull the bone with another. Whoever ends up with the bigger part shares a merry thought."

Planning to let Tim pull harder and win, Bob held onto the lower end of the bone.

Glancing around the table, Tim spotted his brother. "Can I break the bone with Matthew?"

Shocked by the request, Bob eyed Matthew who was picking at the bare carcass. The muscles on Bob's face stiffened. He, along with his wife, knew Matthew was the stronger boy and would gloat after easily beating his brother.

Matthew's eyes darted around the room at everyone's stares. His face flushed. With all the attention on him, he hesitated, then leaned toward Tim and gripped half the wishbone.

Trying to keep it fair if that was possible, Bob said, "On the count of three. One… two… three."

Both boys pulled. *Snap!* The bone cracked evenly in half. Astonished that he held half of the bone, Tim proudly showed it to the family.

Instead of grumbling about the tie, Matthew waved his section of the wishbone. "Ha! We both won."

That brought a round of applause from everyone. Bob tapped Matthew on the shoulder. "That's the spirit, son. I'm proud of you."

Matthew blushed as he asked Tim, "What merry thought shall we have?"

His brother smiled. "That God bless everyone."

Everyone raised a glass and said in unison. "God bless everyone."

The blessing complete, Bob patted his tummy. "Though I am stuffed, I have a little room for the Christmas pudding."

That was Emily's cue to bring out the pudding. And what a wonderful pudding it was. Small as a speckled cannonball, it arrived in a blaze of glory, ignited by brandy, with a sprig of Christmas holly stuck on top.

After the meal and dessert were finished, the dishes were cleared, and more coal was placed on the fire. Bob showed Peter how to make his hot punch comprised of water, lemon, a touch of gin, and special spices.

After glasses of punch were served, Bob called to everyone. "Gather round the fireplace. As we roast the chestnuts, I shall tell you a remarkable story. And every bit is true!"

"And I shall share my dream," announced Tim proudly.

"I can hardly wait," said his father. Holding his son's withered hand, he guided him to a little stool next to him near the hearth where his wife and other children huddled.

"After Mr. Scrooge left the office," began Bob. "I worked hard to complete my work but became weary and fell asleep. The clanking of chains woke me. At first, I thought I was having a nightmare. But when I cleared my mind, I shrieked at the sight of Jacob Marley's ghost standing before me."

All the Cratchit children, save for Tim, gasped in horror, shivering at the mention of a ghost.

"Who-o-o's Marley?" asked Lucy with trepidation.

"Mr. Scrooge's business partner. He died seven years ago."

"What happened, Father?" asked Tim eager to hear more.

"The apparition pointed a boney finger at me and rattled his shackles. He told me I was chained to fear and had to unfetter my mind."

Lucy screamed.

"Don't frighten the children!" chastised Emily."

Shaking his head, Bob laughed. "I tell this, not to bring fear but to free us of the fear that binds us to the past."

Tim tugged at his father's arm. "I understand, Father. I saw monsters in my dream. But Angel told me to release them."

"There you have it," grinned Bob. "Tiny Tim knows what I'm talking about."

"Please, go on," said Tim.

"Well, Marley foretold that I would be visited by three Spirits. The first was the Spirit of Christmas Past."

If Tim had stronger legs, he would have jumped up and down. "Christmas Spirits visited me too!" he cried. "Was Christmas Past a girl?"

His father shook his head. "She was a Black woman with a red dress and evergreen garlands. Little jingle bells tinkled in her hair.

"Did she smell like a Christmas tree?" asked Tim. "Angel smelled like that. And she used a branch as if it was a magic wand."

"My, oh my," said Bob in awe about his son's revelation. "My Spirit called herself Angelica, and she did wave a branch that smelled of pine."

Tim's eyes widened. "Oh, Father, please go on."

"Angelica showed me a sliver of the past when my father spent his money on whiskey and forced me to labor in a workhouse. 'Twas a terrible time. I stopped dreaming of starting a business and settled to work for Mr. Scrooge."

His wife touched his arm. "You did it for us."

"But I resented myself for giving up my dream. The Spirit told me I had to forgive myself and others."

Tim's mouth widened into a huge smile. "Maybe Angel was your Spirit but as a little girl," he said. "She took me to heaven."

Alarmed by his words, his mother quickly interrupted. "I want ye here. Yer not ready to go to heaven."

"But Mother," said Tim. "She told me I don't have to die to go to heaven." He glanced around at the astonished faces. "This is heaven."

His father nodded. "Indeed!"

"And the Spirit of Christmas Present was a little boy like me," gushed Tim. "Except Noel had good arms and legs and a green robe and wreath. He loved to eat gingerbread and that's how he smelled."

Whistling in amazement, Bob stared at his son. "The Spirit of the Present who visited me was a woman, but she called herself Noella. She also wore a green robe and had a wreath on her head. But my Spirit was a bare-footed woman." He neglected to say that she was buxom and bawdy, but he did say she also smelled of gingerbread.

"The Spirits must change how they look each time they appear," exclaimed Tim. "I was told that Mr. Scrooge will also see Spirits." He shook his head. "But I don't think they'll come as children."

"He would get the devil himself," scoffed his mother.

"But Mr. Scrooge will choose love today," promised Tim. "That's what El said. She's the Spirit of the Future."

Captivated by his son's revelation, his father begged him to tell more.

The young boy regaled his family about El, that she had the face of a girl from the Orient, that she kept changing her hair color, and that the smoke from her torch was frankincense. "She turned my hair green."

His siblings rolled their eyes. This wasn't the first time their brother's imagination had veered into the unimaginable. Normally, Matthew would have mocked his brother but, surprisingly, said nothing.

"El gave me three wishes, but I had to use one of them to change my hair back to brown."

Bob playfully rubbed the top of his son's head. "And fine hair you have." He whistled aloud. "This is truly a wondrous Christmas! Like Tiny Tim, I was visited by someone from the Orient, though much older. She called herself Uriella and brandished a torch that smelled of church incense. She told me that our choices affect our future."

"Yes, Father," cried Tim. "We're free to think what we want." He glanced at the metal braces. "I don't like my legs the way they are, but I can choose what I think."

"Indeed," agreed his father. "We can choose fear or love."

The tiny boy tapped his father's knee. "I saw what happened when Mr. Scrooge chose love."

Mesmerized by his son's revelation, he asked, "What happened?"

Tim beamed. "He'll send us the prized turkey." He then turned to his mother. "We'll need extra stuffing. That turkey is as big as me."

"That's nice," said Emily, not wanting to dampen his excitement.

"And Mr. Scrooge brought us presents! A chess set for Peter, music books for Belinda, a doll for Lucy, a sewing basket for Martha, a drum for Matthew, and a box with magic discs for me."

Matthew was about to crack a remark that Tim's brain had gone all soft, but he kept it to himself.

"Anything is possible at Christmas," laughed his father. "Presents from Mr. Scrooge would be a miracle, indeed. Why, the Spirit of the Future showed me what may be—that we could live in a stately residence."

"Did it have a piano and a gigantic Christmas tree?" asked Tim.

"Why… yes," said his father peering down at his son. "Your dream continues to amaze. I was shown a house with a grand fireplace and paintings of angels on the walls."

"And did we wear wonderful clothes?"

"Indeed."

Emily's mouth dropped open. She knew Bob and Tim were close but having similar visions rattled her.

"I want to play the piano," squealed Belinda.

"And so you shall," said Bob patting her head.

"Music books are coming," nodded Tim.

She pretended to press keys on a piano. "I'll play Christmas carols."

"And we shall sing them from the heart!" said her father. When he looked down at his son, he noticed him wince while moving a leg to get more comfortable. He picked up his son's withered hand. "Are you okay?"

"When my body aches, I'll now think of heaven."

"Let's not talk of that," gasped his mother, fearing this Christmas could be his last.

"Father joined me in heaven," added Tim.

Emily's face turned white. Losing her son would be devastating but to lose her husband as well would destroy her.

Seeing her tremble, Tim reassured her. "There's nothing to fear, Mother. Heaven's a beautiful place. It's filled with light and love." He glanced around at the faces staring at him. "We never die. Our bodies fall apart, but we end up back Home with God."

"Hear, hear!" applauded his father. "A bleak future appears when we live in fear. I shall choose a future where love prospers. I suggest we all do our best to make that come true."

Still unsettled by her son speaking of death, Emily changed the subject. "Is it not time for more Christmas punch?"

"Yes, my dear." Bob smiled. "But I have one more story. This one has a happy ending."

The muscles on Emily's face relaxed.

Bob dared not look at his wife when he announced, "I was fired."

Emily gulped. Hearing of death horrified her. Hearing also that her husband lost his job and source of income brought waves of terror.

"Wh-what shall we do?" she stammered. "How can we pay our bills?"

Bob held up his hand. "Do not let fear have its way. There is more."

A hush fell over the family.

"Please go on, Father," begged Tiny Tim, enraptured by the unfolding events.

"I confess," said Bob. "I worried about our welfare, but my time with the three Spirits gave me pause. On the way home from the office, I was about to pass the home of Mr. Scrooge's nephew when I felt a strong urge to speak with him. And so, I did. I told Fred I was no longer employed by Mr. Scrooge. My encounter led to an invitation to join his party. There I met some of his wealthy friends, including Augustus Jingle and Albert Bell. They were curious, like Fred, about my sudden departure from Mr. Scrooge."

"The evil scoundrel," hissed Mrs. Cratchit. "I shall never forgive him."

"The story gets better, my dear," soothed her husband. "When they heard I had been fired, they were outraged. But then the talk moved quickly to another matter. Jingle and Bell wanted a firm that would lend money at a just rate. I told them that lending should help others overcome hardship and be fair and reasonable. Then a miracle occurred. They asked me to manage a new firm. I am sure the Christmas Spirits had a hand in this."

Bob pulled out coins from his pocket. "They advanced me a small sum to celebrate the holy day."

Emily Cratchit's eyes bulged. She plucked the coins out of her husband's hands and inspected them. "They're real!" she screamed.

Bob chuckled. "Yes, my dear." He reached over and lifted Tiny Tim's hand. "My son, we shall get you proper treatment."

"Mr. Scrooge will help us."

No one, including Matthew, dared to disagree lest they disrupt the jubilant moment.

Filling glasses with punch, Bob hoisted his own glass. "'Tis time for a toast."

"God bless everyone!" shouted Tiny Tim.

Everyone echoed the blessing.

"And God bless Mr. Scrooge, the founder of this feast," added Bob.

"The founder of this feast?" mocked Mrs. Cratchit. "The stingy old fool didn't value a good man as ye."

"Mother, please," begged Tim. "We're meant to celebrate Christmas every day."

"Indeed, my son. We must spread love and kindness, especially to those in need. To Mr. Scrooge."

And Billy Pecksniff and Matthew, thought Tim.

"I'll drink for Scrooge's health," said Emily begrudgingly. "But let us give special thanks ye have a new job!"

Everyone clinked their glasses. "Hear, hear."

Bob pointed his glass toward his wife. "To Mother, the loveliest woman in England!"

"Hear, hear," echoed the children.

"Hush," said Emily, blushing beet red.

Bob plucked a sprig of mistletoe from the mantel above the fireplace and held it over his wife. "With you at my side, every day is Christmas." He kissed her, causing her face to flush a deeper red.

With so much merriment, the festivities continued for another hour. They shared the jug of punch and roasted chestnuts.

Tiny Tim then led the family in a Christmas song. *"What child is this who lay to rest on Mary's lap is sleeping? Whom angels greet with anthems sweet while shepherds watch are keeping…."*

Because of the excitement, Tim did not get to bed until the wee hours. He shared his dream in more detail with the family, and in turn, his father shared more of his own visitations. Oh, the fun they had with the retelling.

When the sun rose, the children woke and found their parents wrapped in each other's arms near the fireplace. The glowing embers kept the room warm.

Hobbling to the window, Tiny Tim shouted, "It's snowing again!"

As the family stirred, the house became a hive of activity. Martha, Belinda, and Peter helped their parents in the kitchen while Matthew, Lucy, and Tim roasted chestnuts retrieved from their stockings.

Rap. Rap. Rap.

The sudden rapping on the door broke their reverie.

"Who on earth could that be?" asked Bob walking from the kitchen.

Remembering his dream, Tim cried, "The prize turkey!"

His father opened the door to a man who asked, "Mr. Cratchit?"

"Why, yes."

"Ye have a gift," said the man. He promptly went to the cab and carried in the prize turkey that had been hanging in the poulterer's shop. He handed it to Bob who staggered with the weight of the biggest turkey he had ever seen.

The man handed Bob a note. "All paid for, sir. Merry Christmas!"

After he left, the children and Emily gathered around Bob, their mouths gaping open. They touched the bird, amazed at the size, which was almost as big as Tiny Tim.

"Who sent this?" asked Emily.

Clutching the bird, Bob gave Emily the note.

Opening the envelope, she read: "To the Cratchit Family. From an old fool who now celebrates this special day. Merry Christmas!"

"It's not signed," she said.

"It's Mr. Scrooge," beamed Tim. "He chose love."

Bob stared at the writing.

"Though the handwriting is scribbly, I know it to be Mr. Scrooge's. Tim is right."

"Can't be," said his wife.

"'Tis," said Tim. "He was visited by Christmas Spirits. And now this turkey has visited us!"

As if coming out of a trance, everyone yelled, "Hurrah!"

"Children, all hands to the kitchen," ordered their mother. "We've another feast to prepare."

And a feast the Cratchit family had, one that left every belly fuller than full.

Later that evening, after the dishes were washed, everyone sat around the fire, watching the twinkling sparks dance up the chimney.

Rap. Rap. Rap.

"My goodness," said Emily. "This has been a day full of surprises. Who on earth would be coming at this hour?"

Tim giggled. "It's Mr. Scrooge bearing gifts."

The other children glanced at each other, then at Tim whose prophesies had mystified them.

Sure enough, when Bob Cratchit opened the door, he found Ebenezer Scrooge, his arms overflowing with packages.

"Mr. Scrooge! What are you doing here?"

He laughed. "May I come in, Bob? I must relieve my arms of these burdens."

"Why, yes, of course." He raised his eyebrows at his wife, who also wondered if Scrooge had been drinking.

Never had he visited their home, but Ebenezer acted as if he had been there before. He placed the packages on the table and gazed at the children. Their eyes had grown as large as saucers.

"Ah, such lovely children. Delightful children," he remarked. "And this must be Tiny Tim." He gently ruffled the boy's hair. "Lovely boy. I have something for you and for everyone. The shops were closed, but when I opened my purse—"

"The shopkeepers were all too happy to open their doors," said Tim completing the sentence.

"Why yes, my boy. I was about to say that. How did you know?"

Everyone stared at Tim with his seemingly magical powers.

Just as in Tim's dream, Scrooge handed out packages wrapped in brown paper. And each child received the exact gift Tim had foretold—a chess set for Peter, music books for Belinda, a doll for Lucy, a sewing basket for Martha, and a drum for Matthew. Tim waited for them to open their presents before unwrapping his. As foretold in his dream, he found a wooden box with the word *Thaumatrope*.

He took out a cardboard disc with a yellow canary on one side and an empty cage on the other side. Twirling the strings attached to both sides of the disc, the two pictures merged to show a bird in a cage.

The family *oohed* and *ahhed*.

Raising his eyes towards the bearer of gifts, Tiny Tim blinked away tears. "Thank you, Mr. Scrooge, for choosing love." Never before had he, or the other children for that matter, received such special gifts.

Emily nudged her dumbfounded husband.

"Oh, yes," he said to his children. "What do you say to Mr. Scrooge?"

In unison they yelled, "Thank you, Mr. Scrooge!"

"Remarkable children," giggled Ebenezer. "Delightful children." He turned to Bob. "We have much to talk about tomorrow."

"I beg your pardon, sir."

"I'll see you at nine o'clock tomorrow morning."

"Mr. Scrooge, do you not remember? I'm no longer employed."

"Let's not talk any further about work on Christmas Day. Tomorrow, we shall have much to talk about. Come in at nine."

He ruffled the hair of each child clutching their gifts. "Remarkable children. Delightful children." He turned to Tiny Tim. "And we shall get you the best medical help."

That comment gave the Cratchits pause. The Spirits had, indeed, brought miracles.

"I must be off," he said with a hearty laugh. "I have other errands. More money to give away." He waved his hand to the family. "Merry Christmas!"

Christmas Miracles

My dear reader, as you come to the end, you may wonder whether this miraculous story has any bearing on truth. While truth is shaped by personal experiences, I can verify that I personally witnessed the transformation of the little boy into a grown man, and I can also say he has fulfilled his promise to the three angelic visitors.

There is little resemblance of Tiny Tim with his braces and scruffy crutch with the person he has grown to be. For that, dear reader, is me.

The day after that special Christmas of 1843, my father announced to Mr. Scrooge that he would no longer work for him and, instead, would manage a new lending firm. He had braced himself for the possibility that his former employer had returned to his old self. However, to his delight, he discovered that Ebenezer, like me and himself, had been visited by Christmas Spirits. Oh, the joy the two had in sharing their encounters with the heavenly apparitions. They became lifelong friends. Though rumor spread that it was my father who had caused Ebenezer's change of heart, I knew otherwise. The fragrances of pine, gingerbread, and frankincense would appear when needed, not to mention the delicious aroma of chocolate.

Ebenezer no longer walked the earth a bitter miser with a closed heart. Instead, he opened his heart and wallet to many. He went on to help my father establish a reputable lending business and, rather than competing with him, shared his knowledge so the community could prosper.

Not only had Scrooge become one of the most generous men in town, but my father took our family from poverty to wealth seemingly overnight. Following his dream of building a business, he created jobs with fair wages. The lending company, aptly named "The Christmas Spirit," helped many free themselves of poverty.

Most of the family — Martha, Peter, and Lucy, even Mother — worked in the business and helped many to prosper. My sister, Belinda, went on to become a concert pianist who performed around Europe. As for me and my brother, Matthew, we have remained ever so close. Together, we started a publishing house, Miracle Books, dedicated to sharing words of glad tidings. You are reading its first publication.

I cannot complete this story without talking of my dear Uncle Ebenezer. Ever so generous, he acted like a guardian angel. He provided the means for proper medical treatment to help me overcome my maladies and paid for my university studies so I could receive an education in literature.

As I have experienced miracles, dear reader, so shall you. The heavenly realm offers an infinite variety of angelic shapes and sizes to awaken you to the Spirit of Christmas. Some Spirits come as adults, others as children. Some are invisible, others appear in the flesh. Whatever their form, they come to remind you to bestow the Christmas Spirit on whoever comes into your life. It matters not whether the person is a beggar, banker, or bully.

"God bless us, everyone."

Acknowledgments

Many people have showered me with Christmas presents of support, encouragement, inspiration, and love. It would be impossible to mention them all. However, I send Christmas cheers and thanks to the following people.

My immediate family of my children Melissa and Nate, my sister Rita, my brother Jim, and my deceased sister Marilyn—for all the fond memories of Christmas pasts.

Mary Harris—for her brilliant editing and wordsmithing and for keeping me accountable to the book's completion.

Ahmed Shaltout—for capturing the essence of my ideas in the beautiful illustrations.

Pam Sheppard—for acting as my creative book consultant to help me clarify my message and sharpen the story.

Glenda Rynn—for her support, eagle-eyed editing, and wonderful suggestions to improve the manuscript.

Tamara Cribley — for expertly designing the interior of the book.

Fiona Jayde — for wrapping the book in a delightful cover.

Catherine Clinch — for her creative ideas to get me thinking out of the box.

Linda Ulrich-Taylor — for reviewing the manuscript and offering excellent feedback.

Teodora Bikowski and Kasia Bikowski — for acting as my "children's consultant" on the artwork.

Rita Szymczak and Rich Ostendorf — for their feedback on the artwork.

Peter Gray — for being my Aussie friend and accountability buddy to nudge me over the finish line.

My writing critique group of Rick Morgan, Craig Wells, and Dick Hoff — for inspiring me to polish, polish, polish.

Larry Porricelli and other members of the Southern California Writers Association — for being part of my writing community.

My Toastmaster group — for offering a playground to share my story.

Mari Frank, Brandon Hall, Steve Pumphrey, JJ
Flowers, Donna McCullough, Kaye Thompson,
Tutti Taygerly, Rick Broniec, Arthur Tassinello,
Kevin O'Connor, Michele Lyons, Karina Klimtchuk,
Danna Beal, Daniel Midson-Short, Vladi, Ron Masa,
Debbie Hart, Jim Lee, Anne Moose, Diana Pardee,
Dennis McNicholas, Ginger Szymczak, We-Men,
The We Oneing, and the North County Circle — for
their encouragement and support.

Finally, to my family, friends, and fellow writers —
for continually encouraging me to stay present with
the spirit of Christmas. I thank you all!

Merry Christmas!

"Bob Cratchit's Christmas Carol *will inspire you to let go of the past, awaken your true purpose, and create miracles.*"

— Jack Canfield, New York Times Bestselling author of *The Success Principles*™ and cocreator of the *Chicken Soup for the Soul*® series

The Miracles of Christmas
Continue in the Award-Winning

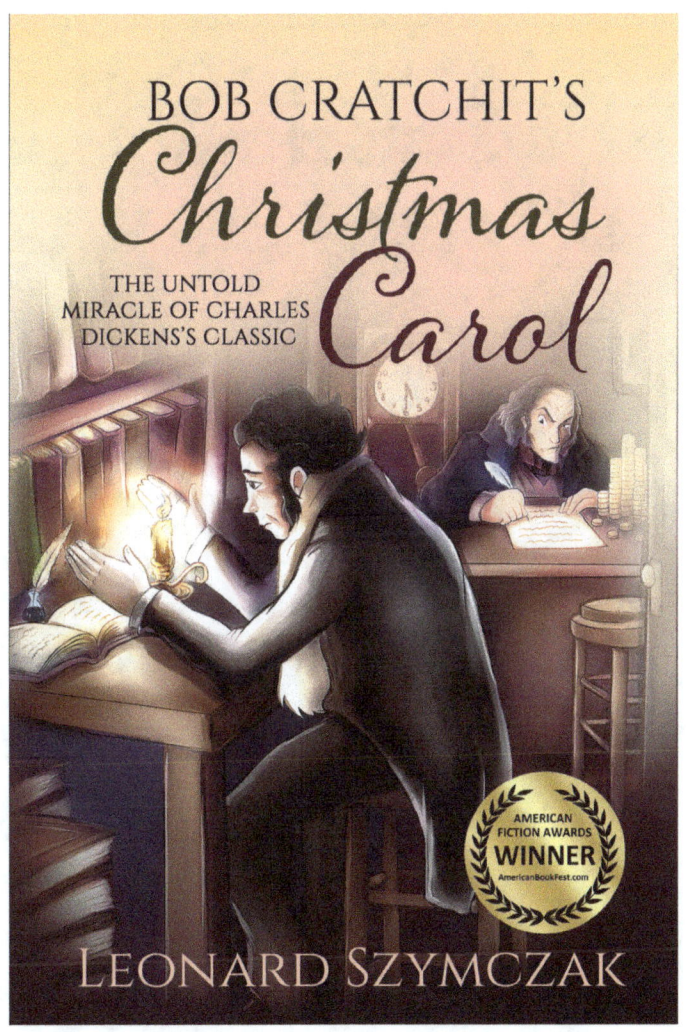

BOB CRATCHIT'S
Christmas

THE UNTOLD
MIRACLE OF CHARLES
DICKENS'S CLASSIC

Carol

AMERICAN
FICTION AWARDS
WINNER
AmericanBookFest.com

LEONARD SZYMCZAK

Chapter One

Scrooge and Marley's Ghost

On Christmas Eve, 1843, in a rundown part of London, a solitary man, wearing a tattered coat, scribbled in a ledger. Bob Cratchit shivered in his tiny office, which felt more like his prison cell. Lit by a sole candle and furnished with a rickety wooden chair and a scruffy desk, the office had a small fireplace. Bob had to nurse his daily allotment of coal which barely warmed the fireplace throughout the cold winter's day. He dared not use more than one lump of coal at a time, for his miserly employer complained bitterly that he wasted precious fuel.

Cratchit, a small man with unkempt black hair and muttonchop sideburns, glanced through the open doorway into the larger office where his employer sat behind a dark mahogany desk, gleefully counting gold coins. Though his fireplace burned with a few more lumps of coal, Ebenezer Scrooge never indulged in excess. He painfully managed his wealth and possessions, down to a bucket of coal. A coldhearted man, he seemed to prefer a frosty room.

When it came to other's needs, Scrooge never wasted. Having his clerk stay warm seemed a total waste. Besides, if Cratchit shivered, he would work harder to keep warm. According to Scrooge, too much comfort weakened the will. He peered through the doorway that he kept open to spy on his clerk. No dawdling on his time.

"Cratchit!" growled the gnarled man who was hard as flint. "Finish those papers and complete the ledger before you leave."

Bob stopped warming his fingers over the candle. "Yes, Mr. Scrooge," he whimpered. He blew into his hands, grasped the ink pen, and scribbled on the page.

At this time each year, the accounting had to be complete before Cratchit could leave for the day. Since Scrooge hated Christmas and paying his clerk for a holiday, he piled on extra work to make up for it. As a result, Christmas Eve became Bob Cratchit's longest day. His wife would be lucky to see him before the church bells tolled nine times.

Bob dipped his pen in the ink and sighed. He had toiled and slaved for the miserly man for the past twenty years. The work had become more unbearable when Scrooge's partner, Jacob Marley, died seven years ago. Though Marley was just as greedy as Scrooge, he had assisted Bob with the bookkeeping. Once Scrooge was on his own, he piled Marley's duties onto Cratchit's growing list of chores — without a raise. The clerk was still making fifteen shillings a week.

Bob had once hoped to be rewarded for his diligence and loyalty. Those dreams had vanished years ago. Though he yearned to work elsewhere, he felt shackled to Scrooge. He had to support a wife and six children, and the youngest child Tiny Tim desperately needed medical treatment.

Each year Bob begged for a raise, but nothing could stir the embers in Scrooge's frozen heart. When money entered his vault, it was locked away until he could lend it to an unfortunate soul at an exorbitant rate. As a moneylender, he was despised for extracting severe penalties for non-payment, no matter how unfortunate the situation.

And situations always presented themselves.

Rap. Rap. Rap.

At noon on Christmas Eve, Mrs. Dibble had arrived for her appointment. Responding to the knock on the door, Bob ushered her out of the blistering cold and into his employer's office. They both stood before Scrooge who, not raising an eyebrow, continued to count coins and scribble into a notebook.

"Excuse me, Mr. Scrooge," squeaked Bob.

"Yes, what is it?" growled Scrooge, continuing to write.

Cratchit nudged the frail woman who smelled as if she had not bathed in a month. She clutched her tattered clothes which looked more like rags. "Ye'll beg me pardon, Mr. Scrooge," she quivered. "I didn't want to disturb ye, but I need to have a word about the loan."

The last word acted like a magic incantation that woke Scrooge from a trance. He dropped his pen and gazed intensely at the woman. "Loan, you say? You've come to repay your loan? You're late."

Mrs. Dibble lowered her eyes to the floor. "Ye know me husband's recoverin' from a heart ailment. Can't yet walk… or work. I'm takin' in laundry and doin' odd jobs to pay the bills. It's… just… we need more time."

Scrooge leaned back in his wooden chair and squinted his eyes menacingly. "Time, you say? The last time you were here, you begged for mercy. I gave you two months' extension — with added interest."

"Me husband can't walk, Mr. Scrooge," whimpered Mrs. Dibble with tears trickling down her cheek.

Bob whispered, "Can we give her a little more time, Mr. Scrooge? 'Tis Christmas."

"Bah, humbug, Cratchit," ranted Scrooge. "I don't run a charity. Having you work for me is charity enough! Write in the ledger that the Dibbles defaulted on their loan. Draw up the papers. I'll take possession of their shabby house."

"No, Mr. Scrooge!" sobbed Mrs. Dibble. "What about me children?" She dabbed her eyes with a dirty hanky. "We have nowhere to go."

"You should have thought about that when your husband asked for a loan. You signed a document. It says that when you don't pay the loan, I take your house." He pointed to the door and glared at Cratchit. "See her out!"

The old woman touched the lender's arm and screeched, "Please, Mr. Scrooge. Have mercy."

Scrooge recoiled at the woman's touch, as if she had a contagious disease. "Out," he yelled. "Cratchit, take her away!"

Bob glanced apologetically at Mrs. Dibble, whose body shook uncontrollably. With thoughts of being thrown out in the cold with an ailing husband and four children, she buried her face into her hands and wept. He gently took her arm and guided her out of the room. He reached into his pocket and handed her a coin, the money he had saved to purchase chocolate as a Christmas treat for his family.

Mrs. Dibble stared at the coin and wiped tears from her eyes. She then placed it in her pocket and said, "Bless ye, kind sir." She kissed Bob's cheek then scurried out of the building into the freezing wind.

"Close the door, Cratchit! We're not here to heat all of London."

With a heavy heart, Bob returned to his desk. How many times had he wanted to shout, *"Scoundrel, sinner! I'll work no more for you."*

To read more, visit leonardsz.com

About the Author

Leonard Szymczak is an award-winning author, TEDx speaker, psychotherapist, and life coach. His books include *Bob Cratchit's Christmas Carol: The Untold Miracle of Charles Dickens's Classic*, a recipient of numerous awards and endorsed by Jack Canfield of *Chicken Soup for the Soul* books; *The Roadmap Home: Your GPS to Inner Peace*, an Amazon bestseller; and the lighthearted satires on psychotherapy *Cuckoo Forevermore* and the award-winning *Kookaburra's Last Laugh*. Leonard is also co-author, along with Mari Frank, of *Fighting for Love: Turn Conflict into Intimacy*.

In September 2019 Leonard delivered a TEDx talk viewed by 100K, "In the Age of Superheroes, Where Are the Fathers?" He lives in Southern California where he writes, coaches clients, and conducts seminars. He is the proud father of two adult children and three grandchildren.

For more information about Leonard's books, seminars, speaking engagements, coaching, or free downloads, you can contact him or visit his websites at:

leonardsz.com
leonard@leonardsz.com
twitter.com/lszymczak
fb.com/leonardszymczakauthor

Note from the Author

Thanks for reading *Tiny Tim's Christmas Carol*. If you enjoyed this book, please consider leaving a review online at your favorite store's website.

May the Christmas Spirit always be with you!

Leonard Szymczak